To
Victor
and the family

from Tony and Marian
Martin
Jan 09.

Sgian Two

An Adventure Story

Anthony M. Martin

Published by

MELROSE BOOKS

An Imprint of Melrose Press Limited
St Thomas Place, Ely
Cambridgeshire
CB7 4GG, UK
www.melrosebooks.com

FIRST EDITION

Cover designed by Catherine McIntyre

ISBN 978-1-906561-23-9

Printed and bound in Great Britain by:
the MPG Books Group

FSC
Mixed Sources
Product group from well-managed forests, controlled sources and recycled wood or fiber
www.fsc.org Cert no. TT-COC-002303
© 1996 Forest Stewardship Council

PEFC
PEFC/16-33-293
PEFC - Promoting Sustainable Forest Management

Thanks to Amanda Burfoot, editor,
and the staff of Melrose Books:
Austin Kehoe, Jill de Laat,
Carolyn Redshaw, Judith Stephens,
Matt Stephens, Wendy Wilson
and Pamela Wilson-Stott.

'…The Love of Books, the Golden Key

That opens the Enchanted Door…'

ANDREW LANG (1844 - 1912)

Ballade of the Bookworm

1

Day One: The West Coast of Scotland

Dark clouds rolled in from the Atlantic. Gruinard Island, dusted with snow, seemed to wallow in a grey swell like a huge white whale. The fisherman looked out to sea from the stern of his small fishing boat. One side of his face twitched. His body jerked violently. He fell onto a box of freshly caught mackerel. He convulsed for a few seconds then lay still. Drowning fish flapped his face. It started to snow.

A hand grasped the gunwale. The fisherman pulled himself up, removed a fish from inside his collar, shook his head and mumbled, "Better get that creel on board."

MacKenzie struggled with the line attached to the creel. "Snagged on a rock," he said. A deep roar ripped the air behind him. A wave of pressure squeezed his ears. "Damn low-flying jets," he shouted without looking round.

The boat pitched and rolled in white-topped waves. The snowfall was now a blizzard. The creel broke the surface. MacKenzie glanced over his shoulder. A giant, swirling black cloud had enveloped the island and was rushing towards him. Something clamped one arm, piercing his Harris tweed jacket, woollen jumper and skin. A pink stain spread up his snow-covered arm. He looked at the creel.

"Gurraiceideach!" His Gaelic curse was lost in the deafening roar.

A black lobster, the size of a wheelbarrow, was entangled in giant bladderwrack. One claw was inside the creel. The other, a monstrous pincer, gripped his arm.

The tornado sucked snow, boiling seas and creatures into its roaring heart. Boat, man, weed and lobster disappeared into the airborne maelstrom. The tornado swept across Scotland. In its wake, dark veils of lichen spores appeared over human habitation and woodlands. After a few hours they descended to infect their hosts. In Edinburgh a disused tunnel under Princes Street and Mary King's Close, a 17th century street beneath the Royal Mile, was invaded.

2

Day Two: New York

She awoke suddenly in a cold sweat, heart pounding. It was pitch dark but she still saw his hooded eyes. A door opened. Light dazzled her.

"Rounds are go, Doc," said the nurse.

Pulling on a white coat and slinging her stethoscope round her neck, the young intern ran from the 'on call' room along McKinley hospital's tenth floor corridor to neurosurgery. She caught up with the neurosurgeon, head nurse and medical students.

"Too much sleep slows the brain, Dr DaCosta." Oliver Jeffrey, Chief of Neurosurgery, spoke slowly with a Scots-American accent. Tall, thin, a grey beard and matching hair, his grey-green eyes held her gaze.

"We had problems with our star patient?" she asked.

"It's a learning experience. Transplanted brain cells in conflict with a tormented mind," he said, smiling.

"He scares the nurses," said the head nurse. The intern nodded in agreement.

"Give it time. He's becoming less volatile," said the surgeon.

"The night security guard might disagree, sir. He lost a tooth and gained a broken nose last night," said Doctor DaCosta.

The team approached an isolation room. An armed security guard was looking through a meshed glass window.

"Problems?" asked the chief.

"Paces about like a caged animal. Never sleeps. Keeps twitching his face," said the guard.

The surgeon turned to the students. "Exercising facial muscles. He can change his appearance in an instant. A feature of the multiple personality disorder."

"Like Jekyll and Hyde, sir?" asked a student.

The surgeon touched his cheek, nodded slowly, then said, "Jekyll and many Hydes. Frin Fregoli was an astronaut and brilliant roboticist. He was stranded in a module that detached itself from the International Space Station with only a few days' supply of food and water. Communication cut off, rescue took three months. He was alive but brain damaged. He escaped from a high security clinic and some of the mission control team went missing. They've never been traced. He was captured. I was consulted and undertook a brain transplant to modify his behaviour."

Looking through the window, the surgeon said, "I'll see him on my own." He entered the room. A slim man of medium height with curly ginger hair stood looking at snow falling past a secured window. He wore a red tartan dressing gown. Books and scientific journals were scattered about the room. One book, entitled *Jacobite*, caught the surgeon's eye. A laptop was in use on a table.

Without turning round, the man spoke in a quiet voice, an American accent barely noticeable. "I had a unique opportunity to study clouds, Mr Jeffrey. They hold the key to climate control. Their power is awesome." He turned to face the surgeon. There was a surgical dressing on a prominent forehead. He had dark eyebrows with hooded, pale blue, closely-set eyes. The face of a predator. There was a white rose in one lapel.

"Where's the stunning Dr DaCosta this morning? Interesting session last night," he said, smiling. He blinked rapidly for a few seconds. The lines on his face seemed to melt away. The shape and size of his eyes altered. The mouth, one moment thick-lipped, became thin, pale and delicate. The voice changed to a higher pitch. A Frenchman speaking English. "Today's young professionals lack physical stamina. Don't you agree?"

The surgeon remained silent. He never knew what to expect from this man. It was unnerving.

Fregoli continued, "Your operation's been a success, Mr Jeffrey. I'm thinking more clearly and decisively. Dr DaCosta told me you've developed a self-replicating, implantable form of the lichen anti rejection drug and used it on a patient in Edinburgh. My plans involve travelling. That therapy would be ideal. She said you're presenting your discovery to a transplant symposium tomorrow."

Jeffrey frowned, astonished at this man's ability to loosen people's tongues. "That case was a crude experiment. I've no knowledge of the outcome. Tomorrow's presentation is based on lab studies. As far as you're concerned, don't make travel plans. The authorities have other arrangements in mind," he said.

Fregoli's expression changed. His eyes rolled upwards. The surgeon was mesmerised. A transformation took place. Lips and eyes narrowed in anger. He heard a deep authoritative voice. "We all have secrets, don't we, Oliver? I know your staff and the authorities are unaware of the source of your transplant tissues." He paused for a moment. The surgeon realised the implications. Fregoli continued, "We can come to some arrangement. I have great wealth. Your pioneering research could make a major contribution to my historic plan."

The surgeon's stomach muscles tensed. He knew nothing about Fregoli's plan, but he realised the significance of the threat. Urgent action was required. Oliver Jeffrey left the room without responding.

The patient smiled. A text came through on his cell phone: 'Travelling to Edinburgh with Nanotech. M. Aboud. Zurich.'

Fregoli sent an email to Aeneas Moidart, Moray Place, Edinburgh: 'Open the Gates of Hell. Convene the Senate. The Pretender will arrive shortly.' He returned to gaze out of the window and said in French, "I wonder if it's snowing in my kingdom?"

3

"How's the nose, Sam?" Dr DaCosta asked the night shift guard as he approached the nurses' station.

"It'll feel a long way better after I've evened the score," he replied with a painful-looking smile.

"Don't do anything, Sam. He's pure evil," said the nurse in charge.

A cardiac arrest alarm sounded. The intern and nurses ran. The guard looked up and down the corridor. He walked to Frin Fregoli's room and entered. The guard was drinking coffee at the nurses' station when the arrest team returned.

"Success?" he asked.

"False alarm. I'm off to get some sleep. No calls unless you're having a party," said the intern. She walked down the corridor.

"I'll do my rounds now. See you folks later," said the guard, heading in the opposite direction.

In the Chief of Neurosurgery's office a pen torch beam focused on a desktop computer. Fingers entered a code and accessed and searched a file entitled 'Edinburgh Neurosurgery'. An item, 'Willie MacKenzie, Poolewe, Scotland', was located. As fingers scrolled through details they paused at the heading 'Stone of Destiny – The missing half'. The item included a reference to a boy called Sgian Dubh who had the 'second sight'. A copy was printed. The computer was shut down. The penlight was extinguished. The user left the office.

4

Day Three: Edinburgh

A frosty morning. A steep tree-lined street. Roadworks delayed morning rush-hour traffic. Workmen filed into a portacabin for a tea break. One man entered a portaloo.

"Ye'll get frostbite, Jimmy!" someone shouted. His mates laughed.

An old tree was overhanging the roadworks. Lichen had invaded its roots, loosening and excavating soil under the street. Lichen spores, transported by a tornado, had infected plants and darkly adapted creatures in its journey across Scotland.

He'd perfected the skateboard fast track while Edinburgh slept. Sgian Dubh, wearing a school blazer and faded tartan trews, rattled down the Mound. His face tingled in the freezing air. Overtaking slow-moving traffic, he crossed Princes Street on the amber. One push took him to the top of Hanover Street. He paused to look at his favourite view of the River Forth.

Traffic jam ahead. Roadworks. One lane open. The single pavement in use was busy. Fellow pupils milling downhill. He saw a narrow temporary footpath at the edge of the excavated road. "That's for me," he said to himself.

A car horn honked. A young woman was pushing a pram across the street in front of oncoming traffic. Before she reached the pavement the child cried. A silver toy car fell from the pram. Sgian launched his board, caught the toy and just avoided colliding with a horn-blaring oncoming car.

"Thanks for that," said the woman. But he was already heading for the walkway. The silver car's image lingered.

The events that followed took place in rapid succession. He saw an old tree moving. He realised that there was no wind. Cracks appeared on the surface of the frosted roadworks. The earth was moving. A silver car was second in line behind a lorry at temporary traffic lights.

Sgian's headmaster was at the wheel of his new silver Saab. He tried to get the Head's attention. A tractor stood on the moving earthworks facing downhill.

The boy leapt from the skateboard to the tractor. He released the hand brake. The Head saw the boy. The lights changed. The lorry moved. The tractor moved. The tree was falling. The roadworks were sinking. The tractor rolled between the lorry and the silver car. The lorry's back wheels spun. It kept going. The Saab braked. The driver of a following 4x4 had an attack of road rage. She honked, gunned her engine and swerved onto the excavated road. Loose earth shot out from spinning wheels.

There was a grating sound. Silver paint, wing mirror and hubcap were removed from the Saab. The 4x4 yumped over the heaving, sinking surface. Its bull bar lifted the portaloo from its base just as the ground opened up below it. The seated occupant, still reading his newspaper, disappeared. The 4x4 nosedived into the crevice. A skinhead biker saw his chance to beat the hold up and followed in the 4x4's slipstream. His bike, then his face, hit the falling portaloo. He saw Sgian and was thrown into the air, shouting, "You're dead!"

The tractor collided with a truck parked on the opposite pavement. The tree crashed onto the tractor, blocking the entire road. Sgian, back on his board, leapt over the widening gap. He saw the 4x4 on its side. The driver was trying to crawl out of a window. He saw something else in the crevice but a howling police car distracted him.

"Well done, Sgi!" shouted a chubby boy running across the road to look into the crater. Fritz Mercet, a classmate, was the son of the Swiss Consul. "Quick thinking, Sgi! Could have been a real pile up," he said.

"Tell that to the skinhead, Fritz. See you!" said Sgian, accelerating away. He felt good speeding towards school. The Head must have been impressed.

Only two images were uppermost in the Head's mind, however. His damaged new Saab and the boy who'd caused the chaos.

5

The man looked at his watch. The overnight journey had gone without a hitch. He downed a treble espresso. From the café window he looked at clouds gathering over the snow-covered Lion's Head, an extinct volcanic vent on the hill behind the city.

"Perfect weather. I think we'll have the coronation on the Lion's Head," he murmured. He took off his soft cap and pushed horn-rimmed sunglasses up onto his ginger curls. He picked up a newspaper and read the lead: 'Wild Nature attacks Scotland'. It described tremors felt in several regions and a 'long-track' tornado that crossed Scotland. There was tree damage but few casualties. A lobster fisherman was found unconscious in his boat in a pine tree one hundred miles inland. He was taken to Edinburgh Royal Infirmary. In the Royal Botanic Garden some plants were growing at an accelerated rate. A cocoa tree produced giant fruit overnight. A visit by the Garden's Patron, the Prince of Wales, was expected.

"Two perfect gifts," the man said out loud. Heads turned. He scanned the second page. A mystery illness was affecting people in the old town. He found the article he'd been seeking: 'The Promethean Power Company opened the first of several revolutionary generators that would give Scotland self-sufficiency in electricity'. He turned to the international news: 'Former astronaut commits suicide. Jumped from hospital window'. He smiled.

A young woman, the hood of her parka framing a pale face and black fringe, sat at his table. "Immaculate time keeping, Pam. Coffee?" he asked, getting to his feet.

"Black, please," she said. The man returned with a black coffee.

"Are our floating surgical facilities to your satisfaction?" he asked.

"The best I've seen," she replied.

"Any problems with the neurosurgeon?"

"Very compliant."

"Good. He sees rich rewards ahead. And Nature's on our side. The tornado has presented me with a two-in-one opportunity. A Mr MacKenzie is a patient in your hospital. He'll provide the treatment I need and the means of acquiring my donor. I have two requests. Provide me with two doses of a powerful, quick-acting diuretic. And let me know if a schoolboy by the name of Sgian Dubh visits him."

She nodded, saying, "Mackenzie's being worked up for neurosurgery. I'll be on neuro ITU."

The man put his cap and sunglasses on, shook her hand and left. A long, low, green sports car drew up. He climbed in. A suntanned, athletic-looking, black-haired young woman wearing red lipstick and a red suit sat behind the wheel.

"Good to see you again, Fregoli," she said.

"Good to be free, Jorji. Been diving in the Caribbean again?"

She smiled. "What's the plan?" she asked, accelerating away.

"A hospital visit, and prepare for a lightning strike," he said. He texted 'The Pretender'.

6

Day Three: Loch Hourn

When ice and hail collide within a cloud, electricity is generated. Lightning is a giant electric spark arcing inside a cloud or from cloud to ground. It produces 50,000 amps of current, heating the surrounding air to 30,000 degrees Celsius. Hotter than the sun, it can turn sand into glass. Eight million strikes hit Earth each day.

Loch Hourn, the Lake of Hell, is a sea loch in the most isolated part of Scotland. Overlooked by mountains, its surface is rarely touched by sunlight. A lightning cloud generator, built into a one thousand metre high cliff face, released freezing water vapour and charged nanoparticles, creating clouds and electricity.

One end of the Promethean Power Company's conference room was entirely window. Five hundred metres below lay the black surface of Loch Hourn. Framed by snow-covered mountains and grey clouds, the distant Atlantic Ocean could be seen.

A motionless silhouette sat at one end of a long table. Four men and three women, all dressed in tartan jackets, entered and sat down at the table. They looked towards the silhouette known to them as 'The Pretender'. Aeneas Moidart, a stocky, balding man in green tartan, spoke.

"The Senate welcomes you, sir. The firing chamber is now delivering power."

Several silent beats passed. The silhouette did not move. Then a voice, instantly recognisable as that of the heir to the throne, spoke. "The hostage will be taken tomorrow. Is the Holyrood assault team in position and the mobile nanoparticle weapon prepared?"

"Facilities on *Britannia* are ready and the assault team is on standby with the weapon, sir," said Aeneas Moidart.

The silhouette continued, "Our man in Holyrood must email the Regius Keeper at the Royal Botanic Garden, instructing him to invite Mr Willie MacKenzie to meet His Royal Highness during his visit. MacKenzie is the garden's longest-serving employee. He's receiving hospital treatment. Our Swiss contact arrives with new nanotechnology today. There is one other matter, possibly of great significance to our project as a power source. The Stone of Destiny holds a secret. A boy called Sgian Dubh knows where it is hidden. He is being sought at this moment. That is all."

A bionanobot is a smart machine that mimics a living creature. Living cells are attached to silicon-based artificial cells. They grow, multiply, interact and learn.

7

Day Three: Edinburgh Royal Infirmary, Department of Neurosurgery

She hated the smell of burning bone. The hand drill she used generated less heat and dust than its electric counterpart. It required great care to avoid plunging the bit into the brain. She drilled four burr holes in the skull at each corner of a four by four centimetre square. A blackberry-sized black swelling sat on the bone at the centre of the square. The surgeon had never seen anything like it.

Intense blue eyes behind a protective visor looked up from the operating field. Miss Jude Wylie, specialist trainee neurosurgeon, addressed one of two medical students standing at the operating table. "This sixty-year-old was found unconscious in his boat up a tree. He had a small scalp wound. Diagnosis, Mr Whyte?"

"Subdural haematoma," he replied confidently, smiling behind his mask.

"My first thought too, but the pre-op scan wasn't typical. Any observations to make, Miss Wilson?"

"Is that black thing a blood clot or cyst, miss?" she replied.

"Good answer. Frankly, I've no idea what's going on here. Maybe someone's opened this guy's head before." She turned to the head nurse. "When I elevate the bone flap we'll scan before opening the dura."

A deep humming sound came from above. The stealth scanner loomed over the operating team like an alien. It slowly descended to within a few centimetres of the skull.

Once again Jude resorted to using a hand tool. The Gigla saw cut through the bone between the holes like a knife through cheese. One nurse irrigated and mopped up bone fragments. The head nurse applied bone wax to stop bleeding. Jude started to elevate the bone flap. She opened the cranial cavity. A black, bulging mass oozed out.

"Scan," she said. The machine whined. She looked at a monitor on the scanner. Behind her mask Jude's mouth opened but made no sound. Her pupils dilated widely. She had no idea what this thing was. A writhing mass of black strands. They were multiplying.

"There's a weird-looking mass under the dura mater. It's growing. Hook and scalpel, please," she said. She picked up the tense membrane with the hook and stabbed it with the sharp-pointed scalpel.

All eyes were riveted on the blade. It pierced the dura. There was a shivering motion. The membrane ripped open. Beneath the green drapes the patient shouted, "Fo bae-huh! Fo bae-huh!" All eyes widened in surprise. Before another word was said, a black wriggling mass shot from the opened head into the air. Everyone jumped.

The head nurse reacted like a baseball catcher. The mass slapped into a steel kidney dish. She clamped the lid on.

"What the…?" Jude's words were drowned out by a sudden whoosh of the theatre doors being flung open. She stared in disbelief at the masked, gowned figure who was walking up to the table. The Professor was supposed to be in America.

"Prof Douglas, I thought—" She was not allowed to finish.

"Returned early for a faculty meeting. I saw the pre-op scan. I'll take the cyst to pathology. This case fits in well with my research project."

He took the dish from the head nurse and turned to leave. At that moment Jude noticed something strange about his appearance. Then he was gone.

"Multiple ectopics. Cardiac arrest, Jude!" said the anaesthetist.

A well-rehearsed routine swung into action.

"Jelly, paddles, 200 joules. Clear!" said Jude. Everyone stood back from the table. Jude shocked him. MacKenzie convulsed.

"Asystole!" said the anaesthetist.

"Adrenaline!" said Jude. A nurse slapped a full syringe with an intracardiac needle onto the surgeon's palm. She plunged it deep into the chest and pushed. They watched the monitor for a few seconds.

"Flat line," said the anaesthetist.

Jude, looking straight at the students, said, "CPR. Let's see how good you are. Sister, prep for pacemaker."

MacKenzie's heart was restarted. His head was closed. He was trolleyed back to neuro ITU. He was awake within an hour.

The young surgeon was perplexed as she walked into Professor Douglas's office.

"Problems, Jude?" asked the secretary.

"Yes and no, Chris. Surgery simple. Minor complication but he survived. The case is weird, but what's bugging me is the Prof's actions. Were you surprised at his early return, Chris?"

"What do you mean, Jude?" the secretary asked.

"He barged into theatre and made off with a piece of my patient's brain."

"You must be mistaken. He's still at the transplant symposium in New York."

"His eyes, his specs and his voice. Even gowned and masked, both Sister and I recognised him." She paused, then added, "There was something...something odd." She continued to think. "Yes, something strange about his eyes. Could you try his mobile, Chris?"

The secretary dialled the number and listened. "That's a first. He never switches his mobile off," she said.

"Try the hotel in New York, Chris. They're five hours behind us. He should be having breakfast now."

Once again the secretary dialled. "Could I speak to Professor Donald Douglas from Edinburgh, please." She listened for some time, gave her number and hung up. Jude saw a dramatic change in the secretary's expression. "He checked in four days ago. This morning when housekeeping went to do his room they found his cases lying open and empty. His bed had been slept in. No pyjamas or other clothes. They're making enquiries at the symposium." There were tears in her eyes. "He asked if I'd like to go to New York with him. He's a bit absent-minded at times. If only I'd said yes."

"I know he can be forgetful. Never important stuff, however. He doesn't sleepwalk does he?" The secretary shook her head. Only after she'd said it did Jude realise the implications of her question. She almost smiled. "So what's happened to him? And who was the lookalike? We need security and the police in on this, Chris." As she picked up the phone another thought occurred to her: why did he take the specimen?

8

Day Three: Edinburgh

"In addition to chaos and damage, you've brought shame on the school! I will provide the police with an eye-witness account of this morning's events." The Headmaster's red face was shaking with rage as he gave Sgian a tongue-lashing.

The Head's phone rang. Sgian, as usual during disciplinary sessions with the Head, was engrossed in the historical map of Scotland hanging on the wall. His eyes were drawn to the crossed swords of Culloden. He heard the voice on the line: "This is Chief Inspector McHugh, Lothian Police. I believe you have a pupil who was involved in the traffic incident on Hanover Street. Witnesses recognised the uniform."

"That's correct, officer. I have the boy with me now," said the Head.

"Would you ask him to come to Gayfield Police Station at four-thirty this afternoon, sir?"

"Nothing would give me greater pleasure, Chief Inspector." He finished the call and said to Sgian, "You will go to Gayfield Police Station at four-thirty this afternoon. Your family would be well advised to consult a solicitor. I have no doubt several parties may sue. Clear your desk. You are suspended. Now get out of my sight!"

Sgian left the Head's office without saying a word. He emptied his desk under the puzzled eyes of classmates and teacher, then left the school.

9

Sgian was stunned. "How can people get things so wrong? I knew something was about to happen," he said to himself.

Some classmates thought he was wacky, but he felt normal. Then this second sight kicks in again and he's in trouble. If only he hadn't seen that silver toy car. 'It's a curse. I wish that surgeon Jeffrey had taken it from my brain,' he thought, heading for the park, skid-boarding on an icy path. "I'm not going near any police station," he mumbled to himself, taking a sharp bend round a giant rhodo bush. He almost collided with his stepsister, Fiona Bellamy, who was returning from hockey practice.

"Ho there! Someone's in a hurry," she said, catching hold of him.

"Oh hi, Fi. Sorry." He pointed to her mud-splattered legs and short hockey skirt. "Hockey in this weather! Getting acclimatised for next week?"

She smiled. "Miss Lawson never cancels hockey. Where're you off to, Sgi?"

He hesitated for a moment, then said, "Willie MacKenzie's in the Royal."

"How did you know? I'm the only one who reads the papers in our family." Then she understood and nodded. His second sight.

He frowned, saying, "If it's true, there's a problem."

Fiona detected a micro expression that told her he was concealing something. "OK, Sgi, what are you not telling me?"

"Need to sort something out."

"OK. I'm listening."

He recounted the morning's events. They heard a shout. "I know that voice. It's Fritz. He's in trouble," said Sgian, running. Fiona followed.

"Gimme that phone, you fat ****! I'll break yer fingers. Ow! You b******! Hold his f******* legs, man!"

Sgian and Fiona burst through the bushes. Fritz had his legs pinned to the ground by a tattooed youth with stapled ears. The skinhead with the Portaloo injury had him by the neck. He was trying to wrench a mobile from the boy's hand. Fritz's tongue was protruding, lips blue, nose bleeding.

Fiona thwacked Stapled-ears' head with her hockey stick. He yelled, stood up, tottered and fell into a bush.

As a child, Sgian was drawn to the thrill of climbing by watching his kitten Purdie. She had a remarkable ability to almost fly up vertical walls. It fascinated him. He acquired that skill and his slim fingers had developed a vice-like grip.

Sgian wrenched the skinhead's stubby, nail-bitten fingers from Fritz's neck. There was a crack. The grip was released. The man roared in pain. Sgian delivered a lightning kick to his shoulder, knocking him sideways. He grunted, but despite the pain, jumped to his feet and charged, head down. Sgian was propelled back into a tree trunk. He sank down, winded.

Skinhead recognised him and shouted, "You're dead!" His Doc Martens smashed the skateboard in two. He picked up one half with his uninjured hand and was about to batter Sgian when a voice bellowed from behind, "I wouldn't do that!"

Skinhead turned his head, then his world turned upside down. He landed on an icy path with a sickening thud. Lachlan MacCafferty, the biggest boy in Sgian's class, feared on and off the rugby field, had joined the fray.

"Thanks, MacCafferty. I owe you," said Sgian, struggling to his feet.

Fiona and Fritz, holding a handkerchief to his nose and upper lip, joined them.

"We all do, Lachlan," Fiona said. She'd 'encountered' him during a mixed hockey match between schools.

"These two tried it on my wee brother. That was payback," said MacCafferty. He went over to the two dazed assailants. "On your bikes, boneheads. That was a taster of what you'll get from me and my mates if I see you around here again." The bikers left. Skinhead raised his hand in a one-finger gesture as he cycled away.

"Coffee in Lorre's is on me!" said Fiona.

"Great idea if they don't mind washing a bloody cup," said Fritz, still mopping his swollen, bleeding lip.

MacCafferty held up his hands, saying, "Sorry, guys, I'll have to catch you later. My dad's asked me to help choose his new car. Got to keep in his good books so I can drive it. Bye." He left.

Café Lorrenzo was heaving. Some of Fiona's hockey teammates greeted her as she came in. "Been giving them a taste of your stick, Fiona!" said one, laughing.

They found an empty corner. Fiona brought three steaming coffees. Fritz shivered, hands shaking. "I'm freezing," he said.

Fiona knew it was a reaction to the mugging. "I know what you need, Fritz." She barged through the crowd to the counter and returned with a bar of chocolate. "This is comfort food. It'll heat you up and calm you down, Fritz," she said, handing him a gold-wrapped bar. His eyes widened.

"You've found my weakness, Fi. Never seen this make before. 'Choxoco. A new chocolate experience. Once bitten, forever more'," he said, reading the label.

"That's the last bar of a sample Lorre was given," said Fiona.

Fritz removed the wrapping and broke the bar into pieces. "Have some," he said.

Fiona knew Sgian was about to take a piece and touched his arm. "It's all for you, Fritz. Your shaken system needs it," she said.

"Sure?" he asked. They both nodded. He put four pieces in his mouth.

There was a commotion behind them. They looked round. The counter was under attack. Lorenzo shouted, "There's no more of that chocolate! I'll close the café if you don't calm down!"

"I've got to have more of this stuff," said Fritz. He was stuffing the remainder of the bar into his mouth. He became agitated. A hunted look. Eyes darting everywhere.

Sgian held him by the shoulders. "Must be a reaction to the fight," he said.

Fiona nodded and gathered up the wrapping. For a few moments Fritz looked dazed. Then, as if nothing had happened, said, "I feel great now. Thanks for the rescue, guys."

"Wouldn't have missed it for anything. Swinging my stick never felt so good!" said Fiona. As they got up to leave, she put the chocolate wrapping in her pocket.

“Sorry about the skateboard, Sgi,” said Fritz.

“Nothing’s forever, Fritz. Helped me make a decision.”

“What’s that then?” asked Fiona.

“You’ll see soon enough.”

“I want to do something to thank you guys. But I need a favour. Could you help me explain this to my dad,” said Fritz, pulling something out of his pocket. His watch was shattered. “It’s a family heirloom. A really old make of Swiss watch. Could you come to my house after school today?”

Fiona and Sgian looked at each other. “Well, I’m free after I’ve been to see someone in hospital,” said Sgian.

“I’m free too,” said Fiona.

10

Day Three: The Royal Infirmary, Edinburgh

Sgian went to the enquiry desk. "Can you tell me where Willie MacKenzie is? I think he was admitted two or three days ago."

The receptionist smiled. "The man in the tree," she replied, scrolling through her database. "Here he is. Neurosurgical ITU. Fourth floor. Lift's on the right."

Sgian waited for the lift. A young woman joined him. "What d'you call that?" she asked, pointing to his two-piece skateboard.

"A plutoed skateboard," he said. Not quite up to speed with the latest street talk, she just smiled, none the wiser. He looked at her ID badge. "Neurosurgery. D'you know Willie MacKenzie?" he asked. The lift arrived. They got in.

"He's my patient. A friend of yours?" she said. He nodded. "I'm Jude. You going to see him?"

He nodded. "I'm Sgian." They shook hands.

"Are you from the north?" she asked.

"A while ago."

"I thought you had a Highland lilt. And what's the tartan?"

"Maree."

"Well, it sure is my day for firsts. Speak Gaelic?"

"Used to."

"Can I show you something," she said, taking a notebook from her pocket. "Mean anything to you, Sgian?" She was pointing to the words that MacKenzie shouted during surgery. "It sounded something like 'Fo bae huh'. I asked him when he recovered but he said it meant nothing to him."

Sgian shook his head. "Forgotten most of it. I'll ask Mum. Is it important?"

They reached the neurosurgical floor. "Might explain his brain problem," she said.

"It wasn't an accident then?"

"I don't think so. Something strange got into his brain." They approached the nurses' station. "Hi, Pam!" Jude said to the nurse on duty. "Meet Sgian, Willie's friend."

"Hi. The patient's doing well," said the nurse.

They went into MacKenzie's room. He looked like a wounded Indian maharaja. A bulky, bloodstained turban-like bandage covered his head. He had two black eyes. His white beard carried remnants of marmite on toast. He was watching TV. He saw them, smiled and pushed his specs up.

"Sgian! Great to see you. And you've met my angel, Miss Wylie," he said.

Jude pulled a fax from her pocket. "Special message for you, Willie," she said.

He read the fax. "Well. Here's a thing. An invite to meet the Prince at the Botanic Garden tomorrow. A farewell handshake like thae old trees that were blown down. Can I go, doctor?"

"You had a close call, Willie. But if it's there and back, sure. We'll organise transport. I'll leave you both to catch up on things. Let me know if your mum comes up with anything, Sgian. Great to meet you. Bye." She left the room.

MacKenzie and Sgian exchanged news of their families.

"Got used to retirement yet?" asked Sgian.

"Crofting's a full-time job. And Sasha needs her exercise. She's not forgotten you, Sgian. I have a few lobster pots as well…" MacKenzie stared into space for a moment or two, then his eyes widened. "I've just remembered. There was a giant lobster hanging onto my creel. Almost as big as my boat. And look!" He pulled up one pyjama sleeve, revealing two jagged wounds.

"Sure it wasn't a shark?" asked Sgian.

MacKenzie shook his head. "And I'll tell you something else. We thought Roddie MacDonald had been having a bit too much to drink when he told us a giant crab overturned his boat. Now I'm not so sure." Sgian didn't know what to say so he said nothing. "How about coming to the Botanic tomorrow. Let me see what time HRH arrives," said MacKenzie, looking at the fax. "Eleven o'clock at the old Victorian greenhouse."

Sgian was thinking of the huge police presence but didn't want to disappoint his friend. "I'll be there," he said.

The door opened. The nurse in charge pushed a dressing trolley into the room. "Time for a change of headgear, Willie!" she said.

"I'll be off now, Willie. But I'll be back with the family to hear about the handshake. Have a great time," said Sgian.

MacKenzie pointed to the window. "You've a battle ahead of you, Sgian. There's a blizzard of sleet out there! Thanks for coming."

11

Day Three: The Swiss Consulate, Edinburgh

Fiona, mud free in her school uniform, rang the bell. She shook wet snow from her coat. Fritz appeared. "Hi, Fi! Just in time for food. There's a reception for Swiss business folk, but Mum and Dad are looking forward to meeting you both."

"Sgi here yet?" Fiona asked.

"No. I'll phone," Fritz said. He hesitated then added, "No point, is there? He doesn't have a mobile."

Fiona smiled. "He thinks we all have a sixth sense."

"The watch problem's not serious, by the way. Mum used to work in a watch factory. She says it can be fixed. This way." Fritz led Fiona to the lounge.

They were still enjoying Swiss pastries with Fritz's mother when Mr Mercet appeared. He was carrying a box of chocolates.

"It's a pleasure to meet you, Fiona. Like to try some of the latest creations from Switzerland's oldest chocolate house?" he said, opening the box. Fiona and Fritz smiled and helped themselves. "Fritz described the mugging and your timely rescue, Fiona. Lisle and I are very grateful. We'd like to repay you somehow. Ever been to Switzerland?"

An idea was forming in Fiona's mind. "Our class is going on a skiing trip," she said.

"When do you leave?"

"We fly to Zurich this weekend."

The Consul hesitated for a moment, then said, "One of my guests represents Swiss chocolatiers. I could arrange a visit to a chocolate factory for you and your classmates if you wish."

"Fantastic. I'm sure Miss Lawson would approve. She's a chocoholic."

"Good. Excuse me for a moment while I speak to him," he said. He left the room.

"Dad will lay on a great day for you, Fiona. Some time you and Sgi must come to our home in Switzerland," said Fritz.

Mr Mercet returned with a ruddy-faced, well-nourished, middle-aged man, whom he introduced as Mr Fankhauser, chocolatier.

"The factory visit is organised. You can turn up any day. I'll give you details before you leave. Mr Fankhauser will contact you in Zurich," said Mr Mercet. He paused for a moment, then said, "Fiona, would you consider doing a favour for us while you're in Zurich? Don't hesitate to say no if there's a problem."

Fiona's idea was now a plan. "What would you like me to do?" she asked, smiling.

Turning to the other man, the Consul said, "Would you explain, Emile?"

"There's a chocolate firm called Xocochoc. The factory is in Zurich. I'd like you to watch this video clip on my mobile," the chocolatier said.

She watched the replay. Two children were given some chocolate. It was obvious that both enjoyed the taste from the delight shown on their faces. A second sequence, timed five minutes later, showed the two children still enjoying the chocolate. The facial expression of one child changed. The girl became agitated and looked towards the person filming. She seemed to be demanding more. The clip finished.

"One girl was given a well-known Swiss chocolate. The one holding her hand out was given—" Mr Fankhauser was interrupted as Fiona held up the gold foil Choxoco wrapper.

"This stuff?" she asked. Fankhauser and Mercet's eyes opened in surprise.

"Where did you get that, Fiona?" asked Mr Mercet.

"Our local café had samples. Sgian and I saw how it affected Fritz," she said.

Fritz looked puzzled. "Wha' d'you mean, Fi?" he asked.

"You were out of it for a few minutes," she replied.

"It was definitely moreish, but I didn't notice anything else," he said.

The men were nodding to each other. Fiona continued, "The same thing happened to others. There was a riot in the café."

"That reaction wears off in minutes, by which time they're hooked on Choxoco," said the chocolatier.

"Analysis of the chocolate failed to identify any addictive ingredient. We need more information, Fiona," said Mr Mercet.

"Sounds interesting. Any chance of a favour in return?" she asked.

The men smiled. "Whatever you want. You deserve it for you and your friend's efforts on Fritz's behalf today," said Mr Mercet.

"Sgian's my stepbrother."

"Really. A resourceful family. Our request carries a slight element of risk, but I think you were made for the job." Fiona was now really interested. "We need to know more about Xocochoc's production methods," Mr Mercet continued.

"Industrial espionage?" she said.

"Exactly, Fiona. In addition to being Consul, I work for the Department of Industrial Surveillance. Swiss chocolate manufacturers guard their secrets closely. We think Xocochoc's been stealing recipes. But something more sinister, as you observed. Our inspectors felt they weren't given full access. I'll provide you with a list of things to look for. If they're charmed by a group of schoolgirls they may reveal some secrets. I'll ask the Xocochoc General Manager to invite your class to see their factory as an example of the new generation of chocolatiers."

"If you would ring this number after your visit to Xocochoc, I'll meet you in your hotel foyer," said Mr Fankhauser, handing Fiona his business card.

"Sounds like my sort of fun, Mr Mercet," said Fiona. She plunged in. "I'll do it. Here's my part of the deal. I need your help to get Sgian on our school trip. He was wrongly accused of causing a traffic incident this morning. In fact he prevented a disaster. He's been suspended from his school." Fiona continued at her dazzling best. "Can you fix up flights and accommodation for the weekend, Mr Mercet? And he'll need a tourist visa. He knows nothing about this favour." She finished with a big smile.

Fritz was taken by surprise. "What? Sgi suspended? That's crazy. I saw it all. He should be given a medal, Dad."

The Consul was smiling. "Consider it done. Here's my mobile number. Call me if there's anything you need. Pity Sgian couldn't make it. I'd like to meet him. Sounds just like you, Fiona. Someone who's useful to have around in an emergency. And I'm sure the truth of what happened this morning will come out. You'll see to that, won't you, son?" he said, looking at Fritz.

"I'll be in the Head's office first thing tomorrow, Dad. But what's happened to Sgi?"

"Something always comes up when he has an appointment," said Fiona. She looked worried.

That evening Fritz became ill.

12

Day Three: Edinburgh

Wind and sleet. People hurried, heads down, along the narrow back lane off Princes Street. Closing time for shops. Lights going out. The tide flowed past Sgian, who was lost in thought. Would he be expelled? What had got into MacKenzie's brain? What did the Gaelic words mean?

It exploded out of a doorway. A shaved head dwarfed by massive shoulders. Arms like tree trunks, hands like shovels. The man wore a vest, jeans, trainers and backpack. He lunged at Sgian but caught half a skateboard. The boy found his escape route by instinct. He didn't know why or by whom he was being pursued.

A woman was gathering up display flowers at the entrance to her shop. She didn't notice Sgian sprint behind her. When 'Backpack' tried to follow she stood in his way to object. She was sent flying through the air to land among holly wreaths. Sgian bounded up a narrow staircase, footsteps closing behind him. He barged through swing doors into a department store. He was on a balcony. It ran round a huge hall. It looked down on a maze of counters piled high with sales clothes. In the centre, a massive jumble of shirts and things, the handiwork of countless bargain hunters.

Two glamorous mannequin figures were leaning over the balcony. Sgian dived under an evening gown. Pounding feet rushed by. His pursuer stopped on the opposite side of the balcony. He removed and opened his backpack. Two black and white spider monkeys climbed onto his shoulders. He muttered something. The monkeys jumped onto the balustrade. They flew in opposite directions, using prehensile tails as a fifth limb. They were hunting for the boy. One monkey saw him and shrieked. The other monkey and the man ran towards it.

Sgian leaped onto the balustrade. The monkey closed at speed, teeth gnashing. Sgian launched the remaining half of his skateboard at a gaping mouth. The skewered animal hurtled backwards, shattering a glass display cabinet.

"Shirts and pyjamas, here I come!" Sgian went from first to ground floor in two seconds. He rolled off the counter and ran towards the basement. Man and monkey pursued. He took the stairs three at a time down to the basement. Dangling spaceships and racing cars swayed and rotated wildly in his slipstream. He collided with a lifesize Lego robot by the foot of the stairs. It exploded into a thousand missiles. Armies of Action Men and Women, dolls and furry animals were mowed down.

"Where to hide?" Sgian's eyes scanned as he ran. He spotted a floor-cleaning machine in an open doorway. He misjudged the height of a teddy bear stand. He fell. They flew in all directions. He grabbed the machine handle just as a cleaning woman ten metres away switched on the power. Sgian didn't see the flex. The cleaner didn't see the boy. The monkey was bouncing down the steps. The machine whined, shot forwards and took the boy with it. It crashed through ancient wood at the back of the storage cupboard then demolished ancient brickwork. Sgian was yanked through. He hung on as the machine rattled down a steep slope. Machine and boy plummeted into darkness.

The plug was wrenched from the socket. The cleaner screamed. The taut cable whipped her off her feet. The monkey grasped the high velocity plug. Door, plug and monkey came together with a resounding bang, crack and screech.

The machine's descent was arrested by the trapped flex. Sgian's hands were wrenched from the handle. He was in free fall for a few seconds, then abruptly his legs plunged into mud. His head was thrown back against a stone wall.

13

April 1746: Drumossie Moor

Boom! Clang! Crack! Clash! Yelling, screaming, skirling bagpipes. An explosion of sounds. Canon and musket fire. Hacking and lunging broadswords. Men and horses raged in battle. Fumes filled his lungs. Icy shards lashed his face. Sgian opened his eyes. Sleet and smoke swirled around. He was lying in boggy ground among withered reeds and clumps of snow-covered heather.

Hands pulled him up. "Are ye alright, Sgi? That runaway horse caught ye on the chin," said a ginger-haired boy wearing a kilt and sleet-covered plaid. Sounds of battle came in waves.

"Where am I? What's that noise?" Sgian asked.

"Drumossie Moor. We skipped school to watch Highlanders beat Redcoats," the boy replied.

"You're Hamish?" said Sgian.

"At least ye remember my name. Come on. Let's get to the action. We might see Charlie."

They both stepped into the bog up to their knees. "Yuk! We'll no get far this way," shouted Hamish.

A horse whinnied. It emerged from the smoke and sleet. The boys pulled themselves up onto tussocks of heather.

"She's come back to say sorry for kicking you, Sgi. That deer saddle and drag rope means she's one of the Culloden Estate's garrons."

The horse stood shaking her head. "She's telling us to move," said Sgian.

"OK, let's go. Can ye ride, Sgi?"

"Never been on a horse. You steer. I'll take the back seat." Sgian rubbed her nose. They mounted one after another. Without instruction, the horse turned away from the clamour. Sure-footed she stepped from one tussock to another.

"She knows this bog well," said Hamish. There was a loud thump behind them. Sgian turned and saw a smoking crater where they'd just been sitting. "It's not only me that knows what's coming," he thought.

Sleet turned to driving snow. Visibility down to arm's length. The horse knew where she was going. They heard a shout and saw a moving shape. A wounded dragoon officer was sinking on his horse in the bog. The horse's head and struggling front legs were just above the surface.

"It's a quickbog," shouted Hamish. They jumped down. Sgian uncoiled the drag rope and threw it to the man. He tied it to his saddle. The hill pony knew her job. She pulled. The boys pulled. The dragoon's horse was being sucked down. Wide-eyed with fear, it whinnied and snorted, straining with all its might.

A whistling sound was followed by a hailstorm of grapeshot that flew out of the mist over their heads and disappeared in the mist beyond. The dragoon pulled himself out of his saddle. Sgian helped him out of the bog. They all pulled with the pony. Slowly, the dragoon's horse was pulled clear. The boys helped apply a bandage to the dragoon's wound. The hill pony comforted the frightened, exhausted horse.

"I'm in your debt, boys. We'd be dead if you hadn't come along. But I have to say this is no place for you," said the officer. He pointed, saying, "Go that way. Our forces haven't started to move in that direction yet. The Duke's infantry have orders to shoot anyone wearing a kilt." He mounted and rode off.

"Better take his advice," said Hamish. "Charlie's over there somewhere," he added.

"You mean Bonnie Prince Charlie?" asked Sgian. Hamish nodded. They mounted the pony and set off. But instead of leaving the action behind it sounded like the opposite.

Swords ringing against bayonets. The crack of musket fire. Roaring and yelling. The noise of battle grew louder.

"Basaich! Basaich!" A war cry of charging clansmen.

"Make ready! Present! Fire!" a Redcoat officer shouted. A volley of musket fire. Cries of agony.

Sgian and Hamish dismounted. "Bide here, lass," Hamish said to the hill pony. The boys crept forwards behind a raised turf embankment. They peered through smoke and sleet.

Bloodstained, mangled Highland bodies lay three deep, some still moving. A figure appeared to one side of them. Sgian thought there was something familiar about the man's face. He wore red tartan trews, a leather waistcoat and white shirt. He carried a sword. It was no ordinary broadsword. Crackling sparks flew from the blade as sleet made contact.

"That blade's electric," said Sgian.

"What's electric mean?" Hamish asked. Sgian realised he was reliving the past. The man had a weapon that hadn't been invented.

Sgian was about to explain when two hefty clansmen rushed forwards. Blue bonnets were scrugged down over their brows. Their broadswords were raised in one hand. The other arm, wrapped in a plaid, carried a targe and dirk. They saw the red tartan figure and hesitated. One shouted, "A loyal Stewart!" They lowered their weapons. With lightning speed and a completely expressionless face, the red-tartaned figure beheaded them both. The strange weapon didn't even seem to touch the clansmen's skin.

"No! No!" shouted Hamish, standing up in full view with a rock in his hand. He threw it at the man. Sgian stood up and tried to pull Hamish back down. The man's head jerked round. The rock bounced off it. He didn't even blink. He looked at the boys. Sgian saw movement behind the man. Two black-buttoned, muddy white gaitered legs strode out of the smoke. A Redcoat rifleman, face blackened by gunfire, stopped on a mound of heather six or seven paces from the man, raised his musket to his shoulder and took aim. There was a red blur where the man had been standing. A loud crack and puff of blue smoke from the musket. The man reappeared behind the Redcoat. The musket was held against a headless shoulder. The Redcoat's body fell into the bog. The man walked towards the boys.

"Run!" shouted Sgian. Hamish was paralysed with fear. Sgian used a rugby tackle to fold him over his shoulders. He struggled to the pony and threw him over the saddle. "Go!" he shouted. The pony understood. Sgian grabbed the saddle and swung himself up behind Hamish. The pony took off. Sgian watched their pursuer over his shoulder. He was leaping from tussock to tussock in pursuit. His face remained expressionless. His progress seemed effortless.

He was right behind them. His arm extended to twice its length and took hold of the galloping horse's tail. She was brought to a sudden, squelching halt. The boys were tossed over her head and crashed head first into ice-covered bog. She kicked with both hind legs. The man's chin took the full force of two hooves. He was propelled back into the mist. A severed hand gripped the tail for a moment, then fell into the bog. The pony trotted to the boys. Except for the whites of eyes and teeth, both were coated in black mud to their waists. She lowered her head. They slithered up onto her back. They were terrified.

Hamish spluttered, "That's the de'il we've just tangled with. He'll be after us now, Sgi. Better get to the MacDonalds' farm."

"Where's that?" asked Sgian.

"That's where her stable is. Let's go, lass!" Several minutes later they reached a reed and heather-thatched croft house with a smoking chimney. They dismounted and ran to the front door. The pony whinnied and walked round the back to her stable. Mrs MacDonald recognised the pony's voice and opened the door.

"Michty me! Who's this you've brought home, Princess? Oh, you poor boys, come away in," she said.

The warmth and the smell of baking relaxed them instantly. Without waiting for an explanation, Mrs Macdonald gave them basins of hot water to wash in. She knew Hamish, having met him with his family in Inverness. She knew of Sgian's clan from the west.

"Your folks have the seers, Sgian. I wonder if they knew this terrible day was coming?" she said. They were warmed through with bowls of steaming broth and freshly baked bread. Hamish told Mrs MacDonald about the man who was chasing them, so she kept watch by the window while they enjoyed scones and jam by the fire.

"Someone's coming!" she said.

Hamish ran to the window. "It's him! It's the de'il!" he shouted.

"Quick, into the cupboard!" said Mrs MacDonald, pointing to the corner of the room.

They opened the door and went inside. She closed the door and went to wash the bowls. Sgian squinted through a space by the side of the ill-fitting door.

The man burst into the house, looked to the fire, strode towards it and thrust his handless wrist into the glowing embers. His face remained expressionless. Mrs MacDonald stared open-mouthed. He ignored her. He surveyed the room. His gaze fixed on the cupboard. Sgian knew that face. Terror gripped him again as the man's eyes found his. Sounds of horses and men shouting came through the open door.

The man saw what was coming. He looked back at the cupboard and said, "I'll deal with you later. The Pretender is my priority." He strode to the back of the house. One after another, three dragoons came through the door. One ran to the back door. Another held a knife to Mrs MacDonald's throat.

"Where are you hiding the Jacobite?" he shouted. Sgian and Hamish charged out of the cupboard and ran at the soldier. His colleague punched Sgian and kicked Hamish, knocking them both to the floor.

"Leave that woman alone!" shouted an angry voice from the doorway. The boys, getting to their feet, recognised the officer they'd rescued from the quickbog.

The other dragoon reappeared. "He's gone to join the rebel chief, sir," he said.

"My apologies, madam, and thanks to you both again." Then to his men, "We'll rejoin the Duke. Mount up!" They left.

Hamish shouted, "The de'il's gone to get Charlie. We've got to warn him!"

Mrs MacDonald went to a wooden chest and took out a gold-handled sgian dubh. "This dirk's no match for a musket, but it might come in handy. Before he left to join the clan, my husband said the Prince would direct his forces from the tree to the right of the Highland line." She handed the dirk to Hamish and took them to the door, called Princess and helped them to mount. "The quickest way is by the path above the River Nairn. Mind you don't go too close to the edge. There's a steep drop to the water. And stay clear of her hind legs. She's a good kicker!"

"We know!" both boys shouted as Princess set off.

The mist was lifting. Sleet turned to rain. In the distance they saw the battle raging. Low dark clouds rolled in with a milder wind. Princess knew the path well. The boys looked down a steep scree slope to a roaring torrent. They were on a slight rise and spotted about a dozen tartan-clad men crouching behind a turf wall. Sgian thought they must be the Prince's rear guard.

"Look over there, Sgi. Under the tree. It's him!" said Hamish.

The Prince and his party on horseback watched the battle from under the branches of a solitary birch tree. The only sign of spring on Culloden Moor, its small green leaves fluttered in the wind. A cannonball whistled overhead. The boys ducked. A second round hit the tree with a resounding crack. It shattered part of the trunk. A thick, sharp splinter of wood plunged into the Prince's grey gelding. It reared up and whinnied, blood gushing from its side. The Prince was thrown to the ground. Princess took off in the direction of the gelding. A uniformed officer and a clan chief ran to help the Prince.

"Scotland's destiny's been saved by the birch," said the Prince, struggling to his feet.

Sgian heard these words. Their echo lingered in his mind. A war cry rang out. "Caimbuels tha tighinn!" (The Campbells are coming!) A wave of dark green-kilted men rushed towards the tree, broadswords at the ready.

"No rearguard these. They're the enemy!" said Sgian. The Prince's escort drew their broadswords. An aide helped the Prince put on a breastplate. He unsheathed his own short sword. The royal party advanced to meet the oncoming horde. The boys dismounted under the tree. It was raining heavily. There was a crack of thunder in the distance. Blades clashed. Men roared in deadly combat. A red flash ripped through the Campbells, leaving headless, limbless bodies. The man waded through both lines and took down clansmen on either side of the Prince. One of the clansmen, in his dying moments, drove his hooked Lochaber axe into the basket of the man's broadsword. It was wrenched from his only hand. The man lunged at the Prince and lifted him up with one arm, then ran towards Princess.

"The de'il's taking Charlie!" shouted Hamish. The boys ran towards the man. Hamish drew the sgian dubh and threw it at him. Aimed too high, it flew above his head. The man needed a weapon. He dropped the Prince and leapt to catch it. As his hand closed round the gold handle a bolt of lightning struck the blade. Blade and man glowed and sizzled. His hair burned. His shirt, waistcoat and trews melted onto his skin. Sgian ran to Princess and held her round the neck as thunder cracked. Hamish ran to help the Prince. The glowing, sizzling man holding the sgian dubh in his hand, his face completely expressionless, walked towards them. They watched, mesmerised, unable to move. The man disintegrated into dust. The sgian dubh fell onto a perfect circle of smoking peat. Hamish picked it up.

"The Campbells!" he shouted, pointing.

The boys helped the Prince on to Princess. He in turn pulled Hamish up in front. "Come on, my lad, there's room for you behind," said the Prince, holding out his hand. Sgian reached up but was wrenched backwards by another hand and saw a broadsword blade flash by his face towards the Prince. At the same time a huge Campbell rushed up behind Princess, grabbed her tail and received two of her finest upperhoofcuts. The broadsword missed its target. Princess turned her head and looked Sgian in the eyes with sadness. They both knew what she had to do.

"Go, lass, go!" shouted Sgian. She and her two charges bolted. The Campbell holding Sgian took out an oxter knife and was about to throw it. Sgian kicked back between the Campbell's legs. He doubled up. The knife fell out of his hand. He fell on top of Sgian. Both bodies sank into the black mud.

14

2008, Day Three: Edinburgh

Sgian opened his eyes. He was shivering. The back of his head was sore. He was sitting in cold mud in near darkness. He saw a faint light at the end of a tunnel. Silence. He stretched out both arms and one hand hit slimy stone. There was a gust of musty-smelling air. He heard a distant creaking, a fluttering sound, a deep thump and a rumble. Suddenly the tunnel was flooded with light. He stood up.

There were small puffs of black dust drifting in the tunnel. He saw huge wings flapping rapidly, darting back and forth. They dropped to the surface of the mud, rose up and flew down the tunnel, carrying a wriggling giant flatworm. A squeaking sound came from behind. A monstrous rat scurried past him along a ledge. Sgian remembered a story of an old railway tunnel under Princes Street. He plunged through the mud towards the light. An uprooted tree had opened the ground. Its exposed roots were black, slimy and grossly thickened. The musty smell was strong. He had seen roots like these in the roadwork pit. He scrambled over snow and earth, glad to see the lights of Princes Street. He emerged from the tunnel close to the Scott Monument. No sign of monkey man.

He saw a cloud of dark fog drifting low over the Royal Mile. His teacher once told the class that Edinburgh's nickname in coal fire days was 'Auld Reekie'. He ran home.

Fiona broke the news when he walked in. "You're coming to Switzerland with me in two days' time."

15

Day Four: The Royal Botanic Garden, Edinburgh

Sgian scaled the high, frozen moss-covered wall along the west side of the Botanic garden. He sprinted through frosted woodland to the back of the alpine greenhouse where MacKenzie used to work. There was a good view of the entrance to the tall Victorian glasshouse. Several disgruntled-looking policemen stood around stamping feet. The royal party arrived late. The Prince wore a long, green tweed coat and checked cap. He shook hands with officials. They went into the glasshouse. Someone appeared with a tea tray. A policeman took it into the glasshouse. The policemen looked even more disgruntled.

MacKenzie arrived wearing an oversized dressing gown, blankets draped round his head and shoulders and pyjamas tucked into big furry slippers. His wheelchair was pushed by a burly, white-uniformed orderly. The nurse called Pam walked alongside them carrying a gas cylinder and mask. They entered the glasshouse.

Twenty minutes later the Prince and one aide emerged. They hurried to the gents' loo. Ten minutes later the Prince and his aide came out of the loo.

The Garden's keeper and staff joined them and they walked away to continue their tour. MacKenzie's wheelchair burst out of the glasshouse and sped to the loo. Pam waited outside. Sgian noticed that the gas cylinder went in with MacKenzie. It was fully fifteen minutes before he and the orderly came out. The three headed for the main gate. Sgian sensed something was wrong.

Later that day a woman walked into a garage repair shop. Her 4x4 was jacked up. She looked unwell and coughed incessantly.

A group of tourists emerged from a tour of Mary King's Close onto a foggy Royal Mile. "Did you see that giant rat?" said one.

"It wasn't real. Just a scary stage prop," said another.

Medical services reported a dramatic increase in respiratory illness. Intensive-care units were full. The effects of the tornado dominated newspaper headlines. There was a report on the royal visit to the Botanic Garden. The Prince was shown tree damage by wind, lichen root attack and shrubs uprooted by giant moles. He was presented with a giant cocoa pod. The Prince's office announced a recommissioning of the Royal Yacht Britannia to survey the effects of the storm around Scotland. The ship would be commanded by His Royal Highness.

16

Day Five: Edinburgh Airport

Fiona sat with Sgian and her classmates awaiting the Zurich flight. Her thoughts were of her father who had died on a Swiss glacier. Frank Bellamy, astronomer with the European Space Agency and convinced that alien beings had been studying planet Earth for millennia, was investigating two reports of lightning striking twice in exactly the same place. One, described in an ancient Norse document, occurred near the island of Svalbard off the coast of northern Norway. The sea was said to have glowed green between strikes. The other occurred in Switzerland in 1531. It was a year of extreme weather in Europe and one of the coldest of the 'Little Ice Age'. Thunderstorms were frequent. Meteorite showers were observed. A Swiss astronomer, Sebastian Munster, saw a green light fall in the Swiss Alps. He set out to find the site in atrocious wintry conditions. He met a farmer who had seen two green lightning strikes on the Rhone glacier. The strikes occurred in the same place within minutes. The ice glowed for some time after the strikes. Munster located the approximate position on a map. When he reached the glacier he could go no further. Its front was over two hundred metres wide and fifteen metres high. Countless wide crevasses made exploration impossible.

17

Day Five, 8 a.m.: Altitude 30,000 Feet; One Hour Into the Flight to Switzerland

"Can I sit beside my brother for a while, Miss Lawson? We've something to discuss," Fiona asked her teacher across the passageway.

"Be sure to return to your seat before landing, Fiona. Keep your seat belt on in case there's turbulence."

"See you later, Vicky," Fiona said to her friend in the window seat.

"Enjoy the first-class perks, Fi.You lucky thing!" said Vicky.

Fiona sat beside Sgian. He gave her a tray packed with first-class snacks. "I said a VIP was joining me. Drinks come shortly. First name terms in this class, by the way. The flight attendant's name's Joy," he said.

"You're a fast worker, Sgi," she said, smiling.

Joy brought drinks. Sgian introduced Fiona.

"This is really great, Sgi," said Fiona.

"No, it's you that's great, Fi. Getting me on this trip's magic. I might decide to stay in Switzerland."

"Oh no you won't. Purdie needs you back home. Forget the traffic business. Fritz saw it all and said he'd tell your Head what really happened."

But the Chief Inspector's words still lingered in his mind. And he already had a police record.

"You don't think I got you on this trip for a holiday do you, Sgi? I need you to do some work." She smiled and gave him a nudge.

"OK. Work sounds good. I'll be a choc-spy too. What are we looking for, Fi?"

She gave him Mr Mercet's list. "There's something else, Sgi. Something I need to do for Dad."

Sgian was nodding. He knew what what was coming. "You mean *we* need to do for him," he said.

"Thanks, Sgi." Her eyes moistened. He put an arm round her. "Brought this along," she said, taking a leather-bound notebook from her bag.

"The Bellamy notebook!"

"I've decoded bits about his Swiss expedition. He'd worked out the landing site of an asteroid on a glacier from some 16th century documents."

"I'm glad the Head suspended me. We'll do it, Fi. There may be one or two probs to think about, though. Exploring a glacier's going to be tricky. How do we dig it out? Then what? We'll need help."

She nodded. "Great minds, as they say, Sgi. I think you've thought of the same solution as me."

"Prof Anna Sterne," they said together, smiling.

"I'll have to get in touch with Mum. The card with her address and number's back in Edinburgh," Sgian said.

"No need." Fiona opened the notebook to reveal the Prof's postcard. "Let's phone from Zurich."

Sgian had heard of travel sickness. Now he had it. Waves of nausea. He said nothing. Fiona saw the signs and called the flight attendant.

"Even pilots can get sick, Sgian. A pill won't help now, but here's one to take before your return journey. I know a trick that sometimes works," said Joy. She tilted his seat all the way back and said, "Now close your eyes and think of something you love doing. We land in half an hour. It'll seem a lot less."

"Thanks, Joy. Hope we see you on the way back," said Sgian. Fiona nodded.

"I'd like that," said Joy.

Sgian's vivid imagination took him climbing within seconds. He left the 'sicko' reclining in his seat. Fiona went back to join the others.

At Zurich Airport they were told that avalanches had blocked the roads to the resort.

"There's your dad's jigsaw theory again, Fi. We were meant to find the asteroid," said Sgian.

"OK, let's phone the Prof," said Fiona. She dialled and handed the mobile to Sgian.

A reply came immediately. The Professor was delighted to hear from him. Sgian introduced Fiona and handed the phone over. Fiona described her father's asteroid theory.

The Professor didn't hesitate. "We'll meet in Zurich within twenty-four hours. I've a friend in the university department of geosciences there. He'll be only too willing to help with whatever we need. I'll call you when we arrive, Fiona. Till then, hugs to both!"

"Wow, she really is something, Sgi. Sounds like we are on our way!" said Fiona.

18

Day Five: Edinburgh

Giant rodents and bats attacked cats and dogs in the streets at night. A plague of monster moles excavated gardens. Trees still standing after the tornado were dying.

A mystery respiratory illness baffled the medical profession. The sound of a cough struck fear in all who heard it. Confidence in the authorities declined. Fregoli could not have chosen a more opportune time for a coup. Holyrood Palace was taken over by the Jacobites. An attempt was made by the SAS to retake the Palace. A nanocloud launched from the Palace created lightning strikes which downed assault helicopters and destroyed a mechanised attack.

Fregoli made a media announcement. But the face and voice on the screen and over the radio were those of a well-known TV Chef. "Scotland has been liberated. The heir to the British throne is my hostage. In his wisdom he has agreed to certain constitutional changes." It seemed like a hoax.

He went off camera, changed voice and appearance and the face of the heir to the British throne was seen. "I have decided to accept the Scottish crown. A constitution has been drawn up. My Chief of Staff, who has just spoken, takes over from the First Minister. The Cabinet will be replaced by a Jacobite Senate. I am about to undertake a tour of inspection round the Scottish coast. On my return I shall be crowned

King of Scotland on Arthur's Seat," he said.

The next image was of the Royal Infirmary. Fregoli spoke. "To convince sceptics, let me demonstrate Jacobite power." Fregoli instructed Jorji to fire a bolt of lightning at the hospital. The effect was devastating. Fregoli, as the TV chef, addressed the government sitting in the new Holyrood building. "Now I have your attention, the following steps will be taken immediately. The armed forces and police force will be under my command. Heads of the three forces and constabularies will attend the Palace immediately." He continued with a series of commands and concluded with a dramatic announcement that puzzled the medical profession. "I can promise that this epidemic will soon be over." Fregoli had no idea how this might happen but he knew the statement would bring the populace on side. 'Chance' would fulfil his claim. The First Minister and Deputy were stunned. Their shaking hands were lifting telephones. There was total silence in the crowded parliament chamber. The people of Scotland were shocked, relieved and confused.

"First phase complete, Jorji. Now to prepare The Pretender for his coronation. We leave for Loch Hourn tomorrow," said Fregoli.

The intensive-care unit took the lightning strike. Three patients were carbonised. One nurse had a cardiac arrest. The only survivor was on a ventilator. Respiratory failure had resulted from the mystery illness. Doctors regarded his prognosis as almost hopeless. His name was Fritz Mercet.

Nanoparticles from the lightning attack were 'inhaled' into the ventilator. Over the next few days they mutated with the lichen that was the cause of the mystery illness. A highly mobile nanolichen was born. It lost pathogenicity for human tissue, consumed its parent lichen, then developed an enhanced toxicity for tree roots. It spread through soil at a phenomenal rate. The boy's condition improved. The number and severity of new cases of the illness declined and eventually ceased. Fregoli's nanotechnology had fulfilled his promise.

19

Day Five: Zurich

Blue sky. Snow-covered wooded hills overlooked the city. Grossmunster bells were ringing. Blue and white trams screeched in and out of Paradeplatz. Snow was being cleared from main roads into alleys. Snow-capped cars were crawling. Steam-breathing people were hurrying.

Sgian watched from his fifth-floor hotel room. He was recovering from the flight. Fiona persuaded him to skip the chocolate visits. But he had a plan.

The girls were standing in the hotel foyer listening to their teacher's list of dos and don'ts.

"Dad said, 'There are no coincidences. Everything's part of a jigsaw.' So a piece of avalanche fits a piece of chocolate," Fiona said to Vicky.

"So what's the next piece, Fi?" asked Vicky.

"Sgi could tell," said Fiona, smiling. Vicky looked puzzled.

Miss Lawson looked at them, "....and thanks to Fiona, a chocolate day!" she said.

They'd been allocated rooms, deposited luggage and were awaiting transport to the first factory. From his room's balcony, Sgian watched the girls leave. He took a Zurich city map to reception and asked the receptionist to point out the Xocochoc factory. He set off to explore the city. He returned to his room four hours later with information and equipment. And he'd remembered to post Fiona's card to their family back in Edinburgh.

The girls were driven to the oldest Swiss chocolatier, which was housed in a modern building overlooking the lake. The chocolate aroma was mouth-watering. After a short lecture, sweetened by pralines, they did a tour dressed in caps, pinafores and overshoes. They saw beans being roasted, ground and pressed, mixtures created, conched, melted and cooled to produce shining bars of chocolate. The workers were cheerful and chatty. Finally, with frequent samples, they watched the creation of a wide range of chocolate products. The girls were presented with a large box of chocolates on leaving. Miss Lawson managed to wangle two!

After lunch they were taken to a 21st century chocolatier in a 19th century four-storey building in the centre of Zurich. A giant gold-wrapped chocolate bar was on display in a large window. A caption in several languages read: 'Choxoco. A New Chocolate Experience. Once Bitten Forever More.'

They were welcomed by a well-muscled Brazilian man with dark eyes and long, shiny black hair. He wore a gold headband, large gold earrings and looked as if he might burst out of his grey pinstripe suit at any moment.

"Welcome to Xocochoc, the ultimate chocolate experience. My name is Zuma. I am the General Manager. Our Director was unable to be here today," he said.

The school party filed in, were photographed, badged, shown to changing rooms and instructed to strip and don theatre hats, masks, shirts, trousers and clogs.

"A bit different from this morning. It's like my dad's nuclear plant. I'm sure these characters at the door had weapons under their arms," said Vicky.

Fiona nodded. She thought Mr Mercet's suspicions might be justified. The chocolate aroma was very faint. Few workers. No chatter. They showed little interest in the visitors. Unlike the first factory, processes were all contained under transparent hoods. As they went round, tiny samples of choxoco were handed out every few minutes. Suddenly, one of the girls burst into a one-minute song and dance routine for no apparent reason. Her classmates were taken by surprise but laughed their heads off. Fiona remembered the effect of the chocolate on Fritz.

"Don't eat them, Vicky. Slip them in your bag. I'll explain later," said Fiona.

"I'm stuffed anyway. I don't know how the others can keep eating chocolate after our orgy this morning. And what possessed Joanne? I never knew she was such a star performer. By the way, did you know she fancies Sgian?" said Vicky.

Fiona raised an eyebrow. "Yes, I've seen the signs."

A break for refreshments. The girls went to a self-service restaurant. Many tables were occupied by Xocochoc employees. Fiona's eyes met those of a young man on his own. "Let's sit with that guy, Vicky. He looks lonely."

"Want to practise your German, Fi, or something else?" said Vicky, giving Fiona a nudge.

"You're a mind-reader, Vicky," said Fiona. But she'd decided to speak to him for another reason. An opportunity to get some inside information.

The girls approached the table and Fiona noticed that the man looked anxious. "Can we join you?" she asked in perfect German.

The young man smiled, stood up and gestured towards seats. "You are welcome," he replied.

Ten metres away a crew-cut man in a dark suit was monitoring their conversation. He spoke into a lapel microphone. "He's talking to a girl about nanochoc, sir."

"The camera's on them. Deal with him. Leave the girl to me," was the reply. The Brazilian called his secretary into his office and pointed to Fiona on the monitor. "Get all the information you can on this Scottish schoolgirl and give me a call. I'll be in the preparation area with the school party."

The two armed security guards came into the restaurant. They walked up to the young man talking to Fiona, said something to him and then, flanking him on either side, escorted him out. He was taken to the main entrance, pushed into the back seat of a darkened limousine and driven off.

20

He'd eaten nothing since the flight. Now he was ravenous. The school party invaded Restaurant Zeughauskeller near the hotel. Dating from the 15th century, it had been an arsenal. An array of weapons adorned its walls. Swiss music, chatter and laughter filled the air. Despite gorging themselves on chocolate all day, most of the girls enjoyed large portions of bread, sausages and potato salad. Their appetites outstripped Sgian's.

Fiona sat beside Sgian and had to shout in his ear. "Glad you've recovered, Sgi. I got some Sprungli chocolate for you. I warned Vicky about Choxoco. The others reacted like Fritz after being given samples. I met my contact Mr Fankhauser before coming here. I'll tell you about it later. How was your day?"

"Wandered round. Ran for a bit by the lakeside," Sgian replied.

Fiona and Vicky tried to give him a description of the chocolate tours above the din. After the meal, Fiona and Sgian stood outside waiting for Vicky.

"Didn't see anything dodgy. A couple of things were strange, though. We met a guy in the Xocochoc canteen. He said something about nanotechnology, which I didn't understand. I tried to get more from him but two characters came over and escorted him out. It took him by surprise. And there was a sign that said 'Bioprocess'. I asked about it and was told it was only for packing," said Fiona.

Now Sgian knew exactly what to do. The three walked by the River Limmat. Vicky said she was going swimming with a group in the morning. Fiona and Sgian said they'd take a trip on the lake. They returned to the hotel.

21

Midnight. Sgian put his scarf on, a Christmas present from Fiona. He pulled on a pair of old driving gloves, a bargain from the Zurich flea market. He opened the balcony door. Muffled traffic sounds. Snow crunched as he stepped onto the balcony. Illuminated clock faces on spired church towers to right and left. Floodlit Grossmunster in the distance. From the fifth floor balcony he looked across snow-covered flat and pitched roofs, chimneys, balconies, patio gardens, air-conditioning and heating vents. A cat burglar's dream! Buildings separated by alleys.

The balcony across from his was at a slightly higher level. His run by the lake had toned up muscles and 'provided' him with rope and a grappling iron from a boatyard. He checked the map for the third time. He focussed a monocular, another market find, on the Xocochoc factory, part of the same block of buildings as his hotel. Narrow alleys separated narrow buildings. He studied the 'crux' of his climb. He checked the route scribbled on his shirt sleeve: '4-metre gap, balcony, patio, roof left, ledge, chimney, roof, ledge, drain up to crux, chimney down to roof, skylight'. He checked his penknife torch. He cleared snow from a garden chair. He tied a cushion to its back using one end of a six-metre length of rope. He tied another six-metre length round his waist. He tied both ropes to the grappling iron. He sat on the edge of the balcony and threw the grappling iron to the balcony across the alley. It anchored.

He tensed both ropes, lifted the chair over the balcony, put his feet on the seat, gripped the ropes with both hands and launched himself into space. The chair swung over. Its cushioned back hit the opposite wall. He climbed up using the rope round his waist, clambered over the balcony to a patio and pulled the chair up. He removed the grappling iron and rope round his waist and put them in his backpack.

The route went well. He reached the crux. If this had been a mountain, most climbers would use crampons and an ice pick. But Sgian had neither and wasn't most climbers. He'd learned the art of flitting from handhold to toehold like a cat.

He started the traversing ascent of the steep, snow-covered tiled roof. He reached the rooftop and 'hugged' his way down a chimney breast to a gently pitched roof. The skylight at one end was locked open but no match for his lock-picking skill. With the torch in his mouth, he climbed down a wooden beam to the attic floor. He saw a ventilation shaft, fixed the grappling iron, let the rope dangle and abseiled down.

The factory was silent. Lighting was dim. Shiny machines, ducts, walkways and ladders, all steel, like a huge clean engine room. A smell of chocolate but no sign of the product. He saw a location plan indicating emergency exits. An area marked 'Bio' was one level up. A ladder took him to that level. A faint purple glow came from a round window in a door marked 'Bioprocess' at the end of a walkway. The door slid open automatically as he approached. He walked through. The door closed. There was an elevator with a digital control panel to one side. He was in a giant, spherical steel space. No chocolate smell. A walkway led to a control panel and balcony on an observation platform. It was suspended several metres above the floor. A Portakabin stood against one wall. It had two doors, one marked 'Ntech', the other 'Microb'.

UV light was focussed on a structure below the platform. It looked like a car wash. Two cylindrical rollers were suspended from a gantry surrounding a floor-level vat. The vat was filled with gold liquid. A conveyor belt was suspended above the liquid. Large sheets of embossed paper dangled from the conveyor belt awaiting gold coating. Metal ducts ran from the Portakabin to the rollers.

He saw the camera a moment before the alarm sounded. He ran back along the walkway. Through the window he saw a large dog approaching. He ran back to the observation platform. The door opened. A large Alsatian barked and bounded towards him.

A man running behind shouted, "Kill! Kill!" Sgian climbed onto the top of the balcony. The dog leapt. Sgian fell towards the car wash. The dog's momentum carried it over the boy's head. Sgian grabbed the gantry. The dog plunged into the gold liquid. It disappeared below the surface.

It resurfaced covered in gold, eyes tightly closed, howling and struggling to keep its head up. Sgian hung three metres up over the vat. He could swing along the gantry and climb down to the floor. But how could he rescue the dog? Its pleading, half-shut eyes, mouth and two struggling paws were visible. A shot rang out. The dog yelped. The gold around the dog turned red.

Sgian glanced round. A man stood beside the control panel above him, gun in hand. Sgian took a deep breath, closed his eyes and let go. He surfaced, took two strokes to reach the dog and held her sinking head up by the collar. With several strong kicks he reached the edge of the vat. He saw boots approaching. The man raised the weapon and brought it down towards Sgian's head. Sgian raised a hand in defence. The hand took the blow. The pain was severe. He hung on to the dog's collar with his other hand and heaved her up out of the vat. She helped with her front paws. The man raised his weapon.

"Stop!" a deep voice roared. A hand grabbed the weapon. A fist sent the gunman flying. The second security guard pulled Sgian and the dog from the vat. Gold mud clung to both.

"My poor Hattie, you'll be alright," said the guard, hugging the dog. It strained to open its eyes. Sgian saw a slight wag of the tail. Despite her shoulder wound, Hattie was able to struggle to her feet. She turned and looked at Sgian. "Yes, that's right, Hattie; this young man saved you. We're both grateful. But how did you get in?"

Sgian told him about the skylight and the ventilation duct.

"And you climbed across iced-up rooftops?" the guard asked, shaking his head in disbelief.

Sgian nodded. The guard pointed to a door beside the portakabin. "Get under the shower. Wash that gold stuff off. Contact with skin can kill. Take Hattie with you. The hand dryer might work for your clothes."

Sgian and the Alsatian showered together. The dog's strength was returning. Sgian slipped a piece of paper towel inside one shoe. He struggled to tie his laces. Hattie saw that he was in pain and licked the injured hand. He'd just crouched under the dryer when the guard put his head round the door.

"Quick. You'll have to go. Zuma's coming. He has a 'shoot to kill' policy for intruders. I'll deal with him. There's a hatch in the roof of the generator room at the end of this corridor and a ladder under the workbench. That'll take you to the attic and skylight," he said, unlocking a door. Sgian ran.

He found the hatch and pulled himself through. He retrieved the rope and grappling iron from the ventilation duct, put them in his backpack, climbed up the roof rafter and out of the skylight. His injured hand was now extremely painful and swollen. He removed one glove and with great difficulty pushed it into a pocket. Now he'd really find out if he were any good at climbing. His damp clothes froze. Every step and arm movement was slow and required great effort. When he reached the crux he was exhausted and shivering. He sat at the top of the steep pitched roof. Frozen impressions of his ascending toe steps and finger holds glistened in the moonlight. His jacket and trews, caked with ice, creaked with every movement.

The grappling iron and rope were fixed for abseiling. Only one problem. His hands were numb, one almost useless. He tried to grip the rope. His hands wouldn't close. He stood up, started to turn and face into the roof. Then he became a human toboggan.

"This is it," he thought, trying to dig his fingers into the frozen snow as he gained momentum.

Whoosh! His backpack was wrenched from his back. He flew off the roof feet first into an alley. He held his breath expecting more pain. Instead, crunch! He plunged, feet, legs, waist, chest, up to his neck in piled-up snow. He blew out a lungful of steam.

Sgian appeared at the glass front door of the hotel dangling his key. The concierge let him in and gave him steaming coffee from his flask, but was so astounded that he didn't utter a word. Sgian thanked him, went to his room, lay in a hot bath and then went to bed.

22

Day Six: *Britannia*, the North Sea

There was a stowaway on board.

"I'm doubly thankful to you, Mr Fregoli. This voyage is a surprise and a first for me and my man. And the giant cocoa pod will give me an edge in the business. It's being propagated as we speak," said Montez Aboud, a twenty-year-old chocolatier and nanoceutical expert. He had short, curly black hair, olive skin and dark eyes inherited from a South American mother and an Egyptian father. As the ship rolled with each white-topped wave, he gripped the bridge rail and tried to ignore the nausea. A stocky, tough-looking man standing beside him was a pale shade of green.

"Will his Royal Highness be joining us? I read on the plane that he's taking command of the ship," asked Aboud.

Fregoli smiled. His guest was in for a few surprises. He'd come aboard before the coup and was unaware of events. "The Prince will see you when we reach Loch Hourn. My staff are in command while he is involved in matters of state." Matters of state meant having royal brain cells transplanted into The Pretender with some nanoprocessors. Fregoli's bionanobot would be indistinguishable from the heir to the throne. And he would have some unique added talents.

A young, black-haired woman walked onto the bridge. "Jorji, meet our guest, Mr Montez Aboud. Jorji is a meteorologist. She joined NASA and was seduced by my robotic work. Now the pupil teaches the teacher," said Fregoli.

Aboud was struck by her looks and firm handshake. His mobile rang. He listened, then spoke. "Did you say Bellamy? Get information. And plant a tracking device. We can both monitor her movement. Get back to me." He finished the call. He looked worried.

"Problems?" asked Fregoli.

"An Edinburgh girl has been spying in my factory," said Aboud.

"Perhaps my organisation can help?" said Fregoli.

Within an hour Aboud had further information and Fregoli's men were searching Fiona's house. They found a gold Choxoco wrapper. The man searching Sgian's room saw a wall map with the name 'Aboud' written on it. He thought it might be of interest. The items were flown out to *Britannia*.

The gold wrapper confirmed Aboud's suspicion but gave no clue as to whom she was working for. Looking at the map, he pointed to the name 'Aboud' written near an island off the coast of Scotland. The words 'Stone of Destiny' were written next to a ruin at Laide nearby. The names 'Sgian Dubh' and 'Anna Sterne' were added. "That's where my father died. These two killed him. And he was searching for that Stone. The Bellamy girl will lead me to them," said Aboud.

Fregoli realised that another of his wishes had been granted. He would aquire the Stone after he was finished with Aboud. He pointed to the map and spoke to the commander. "Set your course for that ruin. We have cargo to take on." He smiled at Aboud.

Sometime later, Aboud received a call to tell him that the girl had made contact with a chocolatier called Fankhauser. "Fankhauser will meet with an accident. The girl later. Programme one of her friends with the special Choxoco regime," said Aboud.

23

Day Six: Zurich

Vicky found a flyer, which had been slipped under her door: 'Free Coiffure with Hot Choc'. "Mmm…just what I need after a swim," she said.

Fiona and Sgian met at breakfast. Fiona saw that Sgian had been busy and had paid a price. "Sgi, what happened? That hand needs attention," she said.

"I got this," he said, opening out the tissue he'd put in his shoe. It contained gold sludge which he'd collected from his 'dip'. "I looked in the Bio area."

"You what? You mean you got in last night?" Fiona's mouth remained wide open. She shook her head for several seconds.

"You were on to it with the gold foil, Fi. I think they put stuff in it that gets into the chocolate. Do NTech and Microb suggest anything to you?"

"Could be nanotechnology and microbes. Better tell Mr Fankhauser and give him that sample. How did you get it?"

He gave her a short version. She was silent. When he'd finished she gave him a hug. "Thank God you're alright, Sgi. But that hand looks bad. I was only joking when I said you'd have to work."

"Looks worse than it is. Fingers still work. It was a challenge not to be missed."

She rang the chocolatier's number. "Fankhauser here," he said.

She told him about Sgian's findings. "Meet me in the Odeon café on Limmatquai in an hour. I'll be sitting in a corner seat by the window."

She frowned. "We'll be there," she said and ended the call. "His voice sounded different."

Fiona got a call from Mairi. It was worrying news. Edinburgh was in quarantine. An epidemic of an unknown respiratory illness was sweeping through the city. Fritz was seriously ill in intensive care.

Miss Lawson assembled the school party in the foyer. "There's an epidemic in Edinburgh. We'll be staying here until it's over. So it's skating, swimming, shopping and Swiss cuisine for us. The tour organiser's sending a refund with compensation," she said to a round of cheers and clapping.

Fiona and Sgian looked at each other. "Let's go!" Fiona said.

24

They walked into the Café Odeon, an old wood and marble panelled coffee house with views to the River Limmat and the Lake of Zurich.

A man, sitting in a corner seat, watched them approach. "My name is Rengli, Mr Fankhauser's colleague. He's been called to a meeting and asked me to take you to his office," he said.

Sgian had picked up Fiona's concern and was on high alert. As they'd approached the café he had made eye contact with someone in a parked car. Sgian didn't like the look. He nudged Fiona. She sensed the danger. A waiter approached carrying a tray of coffee and croissants.

"I've taken the liberty of ordering coffee before we go," said Rengli.

Fiona and Sgian looked up at a large mirror behind Rengli. Two women entered by another door. Their momentum suggested that they hadn't come for coffee and croissants.

"I think not," said Fiona and tipped the coffee tray into Rengli's lap. They ran. The women, two metres away, pounced. The waiter was floored. A man at the bar was knocked off his stool, cup in hand. Fiona and Sgian were out of the door. Sgian saw the car start to move.

"The tram!" shouted Sgian. The 'blue and white' screeched round a corner past them, approaching a stop. They ran alongside and jumped aboard the first coach. The two women boarded the end coach just as the doors were closing. The tram moved. The car raced alongside trying to get ahead. A police car, siren screaming, joined the chase.

Fiona and Sgian, holding straps, breathing hard, watched the opposition. "How far can we go without tickets?" said Fiona.

They both managed a smile.

"D'you feel lucky, Fi?" asked Sgian. He'd had so many narrow escapes in the past few days that he almost sounded relaxed. Fiona had her back to the two women in the rear coach. Sgian was watching them and the car racing alongside.

"OK. What's next?" Fiona asked.

"One of the women back there is talking to the car at the moment. The other's trying to read my lips." He leant towards Fiona and said, "Next stop. Wait till the door's about to close."

They timed it perfectly, catching five people by surprise. The ticket inspector, who'd just got on, the two women trying to get off, the car driver and a man who'd just leant his bike against a lamp post to go into a tobacconist's.

"I'll pedal. You sit," Sgian shouted over his shoulder as they ran from tram to bike.

The women, trapped in the tram, looked angry. The car on the other side of the tram raced ahead to try and cross in front. The police car was closing on it. The blast of *Stadt Zurich*'s horn ripped through the still air. Gulls flew up, screeching. The ferry was about to leave the pier. The gangway had been pulled clear. The bow rope was being unhitched. A storming Sgian and a white-knuckled Fiona were fifty metres away from the pier. They had to weave in and out of a line of meandering cyclists admiring the scenery. The car, swerving in front of a hooting, screeching tram, just avoided being snowploughed. The car hurtled after them along a grass verge parallel to the busy cycle path.

The twin-decked, single-funnelled ship moved astern, churning the grey-green water. The white-crossed red flag hung limp.

"Get ready to jump, Fi!" shouted Sgian. "Go, go, go!" he yelled. They hit the ground, ran two steps and leapt together from pier to ship. They both vaulted over the gunwale. The empty bike ran on, flew out over the water, then dived. They saw the car door being flung open. A man stepped out and was about to run when a police officer dived onto him. Three others surrounded him.

Fiona and Sgian both stood breathing hard and shaking. "Let's go to the saloon, Sgi. I need coffee. And we buy tickets for this trip," Fiona said. They both burst out laughing.

They sat in the saloon enjoying coffee, bread, honey and cheese. "So what's nanotech?" asked Sgian.

"It's to do with gadgets many times smaller than the thickness of a hair. They can be programmed and controlled," Fiona explained.

"Mini computers?"

"Sort of. They can trigger chemical reactions."

"What's that got to do with chocolate and bugs?"

"Might change the taste. Bugs I don't understand. I'll phone Mr Mercet."

They stood at the stern of the steamer looking to the far end of the Lake of Zurich and the distant white Alps under a clear blue sky. Fiona's mobile rang just as a DeHavilland Beaver flew in over the lake.

"Hi, Fiona. We've arrived," said Professor Anna Sterne.

Fiona and Sgian watched the plane splash down, run on and then turn in towards a steamer station.

"We're sitting someway off Wolishofen Pier. Where are you?" asked the Professor.

"We're looking straight at you. We're on the steamer heading in your direction," said Fiona.

"Good timing. Sgian's talent again?"

Sgian took the mobile. "No, Prof, just Fiona's jigsaw puzzle."

They both smiled and the Professor said, "You'll have to explain that one when we meet. See you shortly."

"I like her style," said Fiona.

The steamer docked at the Wolishofen station. They watched the powered inflatable surge up to the pier. Lars, the tall, blond-haired Norwegian who'd faced danger with Sgian the previous year, was driving.

"Great to see you again, Sgian, and to meet you, Fiona," said the big Norwegian, giving them both a hug. They sped back to the Beaver. All three in the stern kept the inflatable's bow out of the water.

"Quite a speed boat," said Sgian.

"The Beaver carries two of these. Great fun on days off. You can have a go after the glacier walk. I'm grateful for this break in the sun you provided, Sgian. Should be a gentle warm-up before the Arctic trip Anna and I were preparing for on the *Rodt Foks*."

Fiona looked at Sgian. "It's the exploratory submarine the Prof's team has," Sgian explained.

From a helipad nearby, Zuma watched them board the plane.

"Welcome aboard the flying truck. The toughest all-terrain aircraft ever built," said the Professor. A slim, athletic-looking blonde came forward from the cockpit. "This is Hela, our pilot. A friend from schooldays and ex-Norwegian Air Force," said the Professor.

Hela gave them both a hug. "I've been looking forward to meeting you both. Anna told me lots about you," she said.

"We've got anoraks and boots for you. And all the gear we'll need. I've arranged to meet an Alpine guide in Gletsch. Ready to go?" said the Professor.

A big smile from both of them said yes.

"I'll phone Miss Lawson and tell her we're going sightseeing," said Fiona. The teacher gave her approval without asking what 'sightseeing' involved.

"Strap yourselves in. Here we go!" said Hela over the intercom.

Sgian used Joy's imagination trick before take-off. He felt no queasiness.

In less than an hour they were over the chalky River Rhone. Hela took them down to view the blue icy vault of the glacier. Serrated cliffs and moraines lay along either side of the vast icy highway. Bright green and deep blue crevasses gaped between towers of frozen snow. "Gletsch ahead. Snowfield landing coming up," said Hela. The Beaver's float skis worked perfectly.

25

Day Six: Gletsch, Overlooking the Rhone Glacier

He towered over everyone, even Lars. Jean Croquet was a terrifying sight. Short, grey, bristling hair sprouted from under a soft cap that had seen countless days on mountains. Its colour defied description. Bushy black eyebrows, a nut-brown lined face, a hooked nose, a fixed frown and a matted grey beard. His eyes were bright and full of interest. He had large, strong hands and he seemed impressed by Sgian's grip. The boy noticed that Jean's watch was almost unreadable through scratches on the glass.

"Happened during a rock fall on the Matterhorn. It reminds me to be ready for the unexpected," Jean explained.

The mountain guide and farmer took them to his old chalet on the outskirts of the village. A two-storey wooden house. Its overhanging roof had a thick covering of snow. Woodsmoke rose from a chimney. Cut logs were piled against the front wall. A big black and brown dog emerged from the neighbouring cowshed, barked once and bounded towards them. It jumped up to greet Jean. "Good boy, Bruno. Say hello to our guests," he said.

Bruno wagged his tail for each in turn, but when he came to Fiona he jumped up and licked her. She was almost knocked over but hung on and cuddled him, saying, "Nice to meet you too, Bruno."

They stepped into warmth and a smell of fresh baking. Sausages hung in the chimney space above a roaring fire. A duvet like a cloud covered a narrow bed in one corner. A tiny black and white head peered out and miaowed. Its twin was playing with their mother's tail. She was snoozing in the master's chair.

Jean's flour and onion soup, cheese and bread went down well. Anna spread a map on the table. Fiona put the opened Bellamy notebook on one side. The Professor studied the notebook, then put her finger on the map. "Fiona's father calculated that the asteroid fell about here. Is it do-able, Jean?"

"Yes, if you don't mind crossing the deepest crevasses beneath the most unstable mountain face and the place folk lore calls 'La Porte d'Enfer'," he replied. They looked at one another with some alarm. "People who've fallen into crevasses there have never been found. I've been on several rescue attempts. Weather changes quickly. Fog or blizzard preceded each of the fatal events. Old folks say the place is cursed, but I'd like to disprove that," he said quietly.

"Did you lead the search for my dad?" asked Fiona. Sgian knew what was coming. He'd promised to tell Fiona what he'd 'seen' but had never found the right moment.

"I'm sorry for you, Fiona. We failed. A strange business. He went down a crevasse during a brief snowstorm. His climbing companion, a scientist called Dr Aboud, turned up several hours after the event and said his mobile wouldn't work. His manner was odd. Almost impatient. His description was vague. But I knew which area was involved. He wouldn't come back with us to search. Another thing struck me as strange. I found a hairbrush with the letters F.B. engraved on the handle. It was about three metres from the edge of the crevasse under a thin layer of snow."

"That was Dad's. He'd had it since boarding school. It never left his toilet bag. Do you still have it?"

"I've kept it with everything found on the glacier in case family or friends come looking. There was no sign of a toilet bag. It was almost as if someone had been going through his things."

Jean went to a big wooden cabinet, opened a drawer, returned with the brush and gave it to Fiona. Tears came to her eyes as she touched the bristles. Anna comforted her. Sgian felt the pain too. He was seated by the fire with the mother cat in his lap and the kittens playing hide-and-seek between his legs. He was holding an old wooden-shafted ice axe.

"That was my first ice axe. My papa gave it to me when I was about your age," said Jean. He watched Sgian's hands moving over the worn handle, then said, “Why don’t you take it out for a bit of exercise, Sgian?”

The boy nodded and smiled.

Hela left the chalet to take the aircraft for refuelling. She told Anna she would wait at Martigny until they called.

They got ready for the assault on the glacier. As they were about to leave, Jean told Bruno to look after the cows.

They zigzagged down a chamois track towards the moraine. A family of marmots scattered as they descended. Jean stopped the team. “Time to rope up. Fiona and Sgian with me. Anna and Lars together. There’s an icy snow slope before we reach the rocks. It’ll give good ice axe and crampon practice for any crevasse work. It’s easier if you face out when descending.”

After the snow descent they clambered over the ice-varnished rocky moraine to the edge of the glacier. Lars looked at his wrist compass.

“No use here, Lars. Iron in the rocks. I think those that got lost were relying on a compass in bad weather,” said Jean.

They set foot on the glacier. Frozen ridges sparkled in the sunlight. A deep creaking sound came from below.

Fiona gave a worried look back to Sgian. “What’s that, Jean?” she asked.

“A glacier’s just a frozen river that’s on the move. The deeper ice layers move more quickly,” explained Jean.

The glacier was intersected by large crevasses. Many looked as if they were filled with snow but most were only covered with a thin, treacherous roof. The route passed by a steep snow-covered mountain face under a big cornice.

“That’s one to watch,” said Jean, pointing up to a massive dull-looking slab of snow. “I’ll be happier when we’re clear of it,” he added.

The glacier began to get steep and complicated. Their progress became very slow. Large clouds were gathering.

“There’s more snow on the way,” said Jean.

They heard and saw a helicopter.

26

Day Six: Above the Rhone Glacier

Through his binoculars, Zuma studied the group approaching a long steep section of the glacier. He spoke to Aboud on his cell phone. "Two men, a woman, the girl and a boy."

"From your description at the lakeside, that's Professor Sterne, the boy called Sgian Dubh, who killed my father, and the girl who's a threat to Xocochoc. Make an accident happen," said Aboud.

Zuma turned to a big security guard in the back and said, "We need an avalanche."

"A spread of four stun grenades onto that snowfield above them should do it," said the big man.

"OK, pilot, let's do it," said Zuma.

They gained height, flew over the mountain face and dropped the grenades. Four bangs and echoes were followed by a deep rumble.

"Land higher up the glacier so that I can get a better view of the action," said Zuma. Clouds appeared. It started to blow. Spindrift reduced visibility. "We can't see what's happening. Better get out of here."

The aircraft took off, buffeted by the wind. The pilot set a course for a mountain pass. An airborne powder avalanche was heading in the same direction.

27

The blizzard hit Jean and his party. They huddled together.

"We stop here till it blows over. I've called our position in to the rescue team," said Jean.

They heard a distant boom. Ten minutes later a deeper rumble above.

"An avalanche is on its way. We're partly protected by an overhang, but hang on to each other with one hand and cup the other over your nose and mouth. If it catches you, paddle with elbows and kick to keep the snow loose," said Jean.

The rumble became a roar. The wind became a blast. The avalanche hurtled towards them at 150 km an hour. It was all over in ten minutes. The wind dropped. The sky cleared. The snow-coated figures of Anna and Lars, still roped together, struggled out of the snow. They saw a leg.

"It's Jean, but where are Fiona and Sgian?" said Anna.

They cleared the snow to find the guide lying at an angle, head down. He was breathing. His hands were cupped over his mouth and nose. They pulled him out. He was dazed.

Lars pulled at the rope that had been attached to Fiona and Sgian. A broken end came out of the snow. "Oh my God," he said.

"Oh no!" said Anna.

Jean looked along the line the rope had taken and saw the top of a black rock protruding from the snow. "It was cut by that rock as they were flung forwards. We search along that line," he said.

They heard the beat of a helicopter.

The slab avalanche had lifted Fiona and Sgian like a huge white hand. They didn't feel the rope snap as it rushed, roaring down the glacier slope. They spun, twisted, tumbled, kicked and paddled, hanging on to each other. Fiona kept her other hand cupped over nose and mouth. Sgian tucked his head into his anorak while his other hand gripped the wooden shaft of the ice axe. Fine, icy powder snow swirled round like a giant swarm of insects. It penetrated every opening. They burst in and out of white light. They fought with all their might, crashed through a snow ridge over a crevasse and stopped suddenly in a freezing blue-green silent world. Sgian and Fiona, covered in snow, continued to grip each other tightly, fearing what might happen next. The tension subsided.

"I'm glad we're together, Sgi," said Fiona.

"Me too," Sgian agreed, pushing back his anorak hood.

They were on a two-metre wide ice ledge. Overhanging ice cliffs stretched above them to a patch of daylight at about ten metres. Below, the blue-green became blue, dark blue then black. Something was pulling on the ice axe.

"Look, Fi! It's as if a magnet's pulling the ice axe."

"And it's aimed at that smooth wall."

"Must be rocks under the ice."

Fiona was straining to see something within the ice. "Let's try to get nearer," she said.

Still roped together, they crawled along the ledge to the smooth wall. The pull on the ice axe became more powerful. A vague, dark shape could be seen deep in the green-blue ice.

Sgian gave the axe some exercise, chipping ice away. They were so absorbed in the discovery that thoughts of their predicament were suspended.

"Looks like a VW Beetle," said Fiona. As a huge chunk of ice fell away exposing a black crust, she shouted, "We've found it, Sgi! That must be Dad's asteroid!"

He smiled, nodded and continued hacking. His mind turned to the problem of getting out, with or without the asteroid. 'That overhang means about a year's work to carve a vertical shaft with steps to the surface,' he thought with a smile.

"What's amusing you, Sgi?" asked Fiona.

"Oh, I was just wondering if we might be able to fly that thing out of here."

"Something tells me we'll be found."

"I think you're learning my trick, Fi."

The axe carried on working. They took turns at exposing the black 'Beetle'. Fiona encountered a lump. She chiselled round it. A long metal object was stuck to the crust. "It's Dad's metal detector!" she said.

"You brought your camera, didn't you, Fi?"

Fiona pulled it from her backpack and took a photo.

Sgian held a finger to his lips. "Did you hear that?" he said.

"It'll be the glacier groaning."

He shook his head. His brain focussed entirely on his ears. "A dog barked," he said.

They shouted.

28

The helicopter approached. An orange-clad figure was standing in the doorway. Jean, Anna and Lars shielded their eyes from the spinning snow as the aircraft landed. Anna's eyes were filled with tears. Lars held her by the shoulders. Bruno was first out of the helicopter and he bounded up to Jean and then gave a wag to the other two.

"We've lost Fiona and Sgian," said Jean.

"There's still time, Jean," said the orange-clad figure. Two other mountain guides were unloading search gear and a stretcher sledge.

"What direction, Jean?" asked 'orange' man. Jean pointed to the exposed black rock.

The search party set off. The aircraft would stay in position until required. The pilot and winchman remained on board.

"Go find them, Bruno," said Jean. Bruno already knew who was missing and whose scent he sought. Half an hour and 300 metres further on, Bruno picked up the scent and ran.

Lars was looking at his wrist compass. "Something strange going on here. The needle's going crazy," he said. Jean was nodding. They all gathered round. The compass needle was oscillating and dipping forcibly, then twirling round.

"I've never seen magnetite rocks have such powerful effects," said the Professor.

Bruno stopped suddenly. He gave two short, sharp barks. Hair on his back bristled. He looked back at Jean. "Bruno's found a crevasse. The way your compass is behaving suggests we're near La Porte d'Enfer," he said.

They heard faint sounds. Jean walked forwards, slowly prodding the snow with his ice axe. A snow bridge disappeared, exposing a huge crevasse, La Porte d'Enfer. Bruno was at his side looking up at him, wagging his tail. Jean and Bruno knew they'd found the two. Jean called out, "Sgian, Fiona, can you hear me?"

"We're alright. About ten metres down on a ledge. And we've found it!" shouted Sgian.

The rescue team set up a rescue pulley. Jean abseiled down to them with tears in his eyes. They were safe. It was the first time anyone had survived a fall into La Porte d'Enfer. It was the end of the fearful legend. All three hugged. Fiona pointed to the black VW shape. Sgian showed him the effect on the ice axe. Jean looked at his compass. The needle was quivering and pulled towards the object.

He fitted them both with harnesses and they were lifted out into bright sunshine in a blue sky on a frozen snowscape.

Two big, black birds circled above the group calling, "Skree, skree, skree."

"They know you, Sgi," said Fiona, pointing to them.

"These are Alpine choughs. Very tough birds," said Jean.

Fiona was welcomed at the top by wet kisses from Bruno and hugs all around.

The Professor abseiled down to take photos, then phoned her colleague Dr Vogelsanger in Zurich. He set wheels in motion immediately. This was a unique find. It would be extracted from the glacier that day. The Swiss army had been on standby since the Professor had discussed the expedition with the geoscientist earlier.

The lucky, exhausted, successful party returned by helicopter to Gletsch. Hela flew back from Martigny. Fiona and Anna prepared massive omelettes and tomato salad. They toasted each other with Jean's special red kirsch, Fiona and Sgian taking it on sugar lumps. Then they bade farewell to Jean, Bruno and the black and white cat family. The mountains and glacier had bound them together in a unique friendship.

A team arrived from the geophysics department of Zurich University. Assisted by Swiss army engineers, they excavated the asteroid. The black, encrusted 'VW Beetle' was transported by Chinook helicopter to the university for examination. The Beaver followed.

29

Day Six: *Britannia*, Gruinard Bay

The ship dropped anchor opposite the ruined chapel. Fregoli, Jorji, several mercenaries and a red robot went ashore by launch. They dismantled the ruin stone by stone and found the large piece of the Stone of Destiny with its gold attachment.

"I want to take a look at Gruinard Island. It has a reputation," said Fregoli.

They reached the island by launch. Jorji stopped on the beach and looked around. "Have you noticed there are no birds flying over the island? They all seem to veer away when they come within half a kilometre," she said. She stripped off, revealing a red wet suit. "I'm going to see if the fish have the same aversion."

"Take the bot with you to keep watch," said Fregoli.

Jorji and the robot went over to a headland and she dived in. Fregoli and the mercenaries walked over a deserted heath. They came to a ruin. A sign read 'Gruinard Monastery'.

One mercenary clambered over the stone blocks and looked inside. He whistled. "This you gotta see, sir."

Fregoli and the others joined him. They looked down into a seemingly bottomless black crater. The mercenary shone a torch. It was as if the beam were shining at the night sky.

"What's that? Something moved," said Fregoli, pointing. The

mercenary moved the beam. About ten metres down from the top there was a rippling movement. “Welcome to the ‘Lost World’. That wall’s covered with giant bats bigger than swans. I think this place needs investigation. But for now I’ve no wish to know if they like human blood. Let’s go!”

Jorji was standing on the headland, looking at the beach.

“See anything interesting?” said Fregoli as he approached.

“What do you make of that?” She pointed to a headless robot lying on the shore. “It was standing on the shore monitoring my dive as I submerged. I didn’t look again until I was coming out. No sign of the head anywhere. Oh and I found this on a bony hand on the bottom. Not one fish anywhere.” She handed him a ring.

He looked at the gold ring. “O.A. That might just be our guest’s father’s ring.” He told the mercenaries to bring the headless robot to the launch. “Something very strange is going on here. Back to the ship.”

Back on board they tried every which way to remove the gold sgian from the Stone, but failed. As Fregoli examined the Stone’s surface he remembered something.

“Now I understand the item on Oliver Jeffrey’s computer: ‘Stone of Destiny, the missing half’. The boy Sgian Dubh has the information. He must be found,” he said.

Montez Aboud was still recovering from nausea in his cabin. He felt a sense of achievement knowing that his father’s death had been avenged and the threat to his business removed.

30

Day Six: Zurich University

"The outer fusion crust is about half a metre thick. It's made of space debris-type minerals. Beneath that it's a completely different matter. We pulverised several diamond bits trying to drill out a sample. Eventually we got some stuff. It's a weird polymer of carbon and an isotope of gold," said Dr Vogelsanger. The three Norwegians and two Scots were seated round a table in his room.

The Professor and Sgian looked at each other and said in unison, "The gold sgian!"

"What does that mean?" asked the Doctor.

"The Stone of Destiny was found in a meteorite. It broke in two. A large piece has a dagger-shaped gold attachment which Sgian and I call the gold sgian. It's hidden in a ruined chapel in Scotland. The whereabouts of the other piece is a mystery. They're made of minerals and carbon with unique crystalline structures. I'm sure they're from the same place as the asteroid," said the Professor.

"We've dated it to about 2000 years ago. If this thing landed in 1531, that means it may have been travelling in space for about 500 years," said the Doctor. "Now we come to the pièce de résistance." His voice quivered with emotion. "It's like a dream. Take a deep breath and prepare yourselves for a shock. Come with me," he said, leading them through to a laboratory. They gathered round a huge transparent cabinet. He switched on a spotlight. The black 'Beetle' was now like a partially open chestnut. "We've removed a section of crust." A shining gold surface was visible. He swung a large lens over the gap in the crust. "Look and be amazed!" he said.

"Fiona, you first. It's the Bellamy find," said the Professor.

One after another they looked through the lens. Only Fiona found words. "Dad was right. There are others out there." There were tears in her eyes. Sgian put his arm round her. The others looked at the doctor in stunned silence.

"Now we'll remove the entire crust," said Dr Vogelsanger.

Fiona and the Professor requested laptops. Fiona found a Latin site. The Professor caught up on world news. "The Prince of Wales kidnapped. Terrorists in Edinburgh and an epidemic in Scotland," she said.

Sgian, looking over her shoulder, thought of the face he'd seen in the Botanic garden.

Three hours and cups of coffee later, Dr Vogelsanger took them back to the lab. "We've removed the entire crust. Now all we need is a Latin scholar. Any offers?" he said.

"I'll have a go," said Fiona. She read it to herself first. "I don't think my Latin teacher would approve of the way it's written. Nor my translation. But here goes anyway." She read the words out loud: "Tabellarius lapis Ianuarius aurum et saxum fulmine ictus exterminare corpus niger ad vitum revocare." Her pronunciation was perfect. "I think it means 'Messenger stone Ianuarius, gold and rock struck by lightning, banish black matter to restore life'."

Vogelsanger was on the net. "Ianuarius, a planet in a distant solar system. Named after the God Janus who had two faces. One to do with beginnings, the other to do with endings," he said.

"Banish black matter. It's just struck me," said the Professor. "That epidemic in Scotland is thought to be caused by an unknown species of black lichen. Humans and trees are being attacked. We've seen that stuff before, haven't we, Sgian?"

He nodded. "The black stuff on the island. When I was about to have my brain explored I heard the surgeon tell his assistant that Dr Aboud had provided him with a lichen drug."

"And Aboud was an astrochemist. He worked with my dad on satellites. He analysed materials after they'd been in space. Something strange happened to the Foton mission satellite. My dad said it encountered a dust cloud. Maybe the black lichen had invaded it and Aboud secretly stored it,"said Fiona.

"And this message was an advance warning," said the Professor.

"But if it was sent 2000 years ago, why has it taken the invader so long to get here?" said Dr Vogelsanger.

"Maybe the message went to several solar systems. A sort of mail shot. And the lichen's infecting planets one after the other," said Fiona.

"And we're the lucky ones to have been sent the Stone of Destiny," said Sgian.

"I like that hypothesis," said the Doctor. The Professor nodded in agreement. "So your Stone of Destiny plus lightning will defeat the black invader. Sounds like a historic battle."

The words triggered an image in Sgian's mind. Bonnie Prince Charlie standing under a tree saying, "Scotland's destiny has been saved by a birch."

"I hope so, Vogie. The only problem is we've only got one piece of Stone," said the Professor.

"I've just thought of a place MacKenzie might have hidden the piece," said Sgian. The Professor and Fiona smiled.

"The asteroid's all yours now, Vogie. If Sgian has a hunch, we follow it. Come on, team. Time to fly!" the Professor said.

They thanked the Doctor who said that he'd speak to the Professor before releasing details to the press.

That evening they flew to the north west of Scotland.

31

Day Seven: Gruinard Bay

The Beaver landed at night. They slept on board. Hela prepared an early breakfast. She remained on the plane while the others went ashore to remove the Stone and gold sgian from the wall of the ruined chapel. They found a pile of rubble. Lars got busy moving stones.

"The tornado must have done this," said the Professor.

"Or someone else has been here," said Sgian. "Can I follow the hunch, Prof?"

During the flight, Sgian had told them about MacKenzie's Gaelic words during his operation and how Mairi had thought it sounded like the word for 'birch'. "Maybe he hid the piece of Stone under the one he planted in Inverewe garden in 1950," he said.

"How big do you think the piece is, Anna?" asked Fiona.

"It took two of us to carry the gold sgian piece," said Lars.

"And presumably MacKenzie carried the other piece on his own," said the Professor.

"It'll probably fit in my backpack, Sgian. It's yours now," said Fiona, handing over her bag.

"Go to it, Sgian. You and Hela can fly round to Loch Ewe," said the Professor.

"When we've got the whole Stone, what do you plan doing with it?"

Lars asked the Professor.

"To be frank, I don't know. Somehow we have to catch a bolt of lightning. But remembering what happened to our Viking ancestor, it may trigger an earthquake. I think we'll need the help of a physicist."

Lars ferried Sgian to the Beaver.

32

Day Seven: Loch Ewe

The Beaver landed on Loch Ewe. Sgian and Hela stepped ashore from the inflatable.

"We'll see how MacKenzie is since he got out of hospital and if he can remember anything about the hiding place of the Stone," said Sgian.

MacKenzie's memory was no better. They enjoyed his mother's scones and tea while MacKenzie told them about the Royal Yacht's visit.

"Did it go near the ruin at Laide?" asked Sgian.

"So I heard. The Prince is interested in architecture, isn't he," said MacKenzie.

"He'll be providing funds to have it rebuilt, I suppose," said Sgian.

Mrs MacKenzie shook her head. "The strangest thing, Sgian. The ruin was the only building not touched by the tornado." Hela and Sgian nodded to each other.

"And something else. The only tree left standing in the Botanic Garden was the Inverewe birch I planted all those years ago. Morag MacDonald used to say it was evergreen because of my green fingers. But I used to always say it had enchanted roots," said MacKenzie, smiling.

Sgian's hunch was being confirmed. They left, promising to return.

33

Day Seven: Loch Hourn

Britannia sailed into Loch Hourn just before dawn. She berthed at a pier in sight of the floodlit Promethean Power Project. Fregoli and Aboud stood by the stern rail. The chocolatier continuously fiddled with his father's gold ring, now on a live finger again. He was desperate to be out of this place.

Fregoli pointed to the lightning generator. An open vertical shaft had been carved out of the mountain from lochside to mountaintop. A tall lightning conductor stood on the summit. Fixed ladders and an elevator ran alongside. There was a building at the base. A cage was suspended a hundred metres up beside the shaft.

"That's the firing chamber. It houses a gun that fires supercooled water and shells loaded with charged nanoparticles up the shaft into the cloud created. The particles are controlled by computer so we can focus the lighning bolt. It shoots back down the shaft and a diamond mirror reflects the lightning to a power unit. I've put the Stone and gold in there. A piece of the Stone is missing, but not for long. Then we'll investigate its properties," said Fregoli.

"And the cage?" asked Aboud.

"That's the Faraday cage. It protects my maintenance crew against lightning. Now if you'll excuse me, my other guest, Professor Douglas, has to implant medication in my head. Then we'll open His Royal

Highness's head."

Aboud thought he misheard and just nodded. Then he thought again, opened his mouth but couldn't speak. The colour drained from his face.

Fregoli saw the shocked expression and smiled. He turned to go and added, "By the way, I'm giving some of my staff a couple of days off. We'll be looked after by bots." Aboud had no idea what that meant.

He'd dozed off in his cabin. A familiar voice called his name. His voice. Aboud thought he was having a nightmare. Then he realised his eyes were open. The figure was two metres high. The head, like a white rugby ball on its side, sat on a long neck of metal rings. The torso was egg-shaped with four arms and two legs. A giant, upright white ant looked down at him with one oval eye.

"I am your steward, Mr Aboud," said the robot, exactly mimicking his voice.

Aboud was speechless. Fregoli walked in with a surgical dressing on his head. "Feeling better?" he asked. He saw fear on his guest's face. "Ah, galleybot's introduced itself?" Aboud nodded.

Aboud's man entered, thought his master was being threatened and drew his handgun.

"No, no, Coia. Put that away!" said Aboud.

"Let me explain," Fregoli said. "The crew consists of four officers. The commander, navigator, engineer and chef are all from the MacRahannish clan. There are ten robots. The white stewardbot, two black and white galleybots, one blue stokerbot and six red marinebots, one of which has lost its head. Different from *Britannia*'s previous complement of twenty officers and two hundred and twenty men. I also have several mercenaries on board."

"But the voice?" said Aboud.

"They're programmed to store and respond to sounds. Our conversation on the bridge built up a voice print," explained Fregoli.

Aboud was recovering but still felt insecure. He was frightened. "I never thanked you for your help with that spying girl. My team in Switzerland have dealt with her and the two who were responsible for my father's death," he said, hoping to please his host. However, these words had the opposite effect.

Fregoli blinked rapidly several times. His lips curled. His eyes narrowed. A black look confronted a quivering Aboud. A deep hollow voice spoke. "Just run that by me again, Mr Aboud."

Aboud's bladder control gave way as he repeated the statement, stuttering.

Fregoli spoke slowly again. His tone was threatening. "I hope your team was unsuccessful, for your sake. The secret of the Stone of Destiny is known by only two people on this planet. Who do you do think they are, Mr Aboud?"

Fregoli left the cabin. He summoned Commander MacRahannish. "Send four men to Poolewe at once. This man knows the whereabouts of part of the Stone of Destiny. Use the Inquisitor to get that information. It must be done in a location where no trace of remains will be found," he said, handing him a photograph of MacKenzie with a name and address written on the back. "This will be the third time MacKenzie has assisted me. Such a contrast to my small-brained guest." The commander left.

Aboud, now almost paralysed with fear, changed his trousers and made several calls to Switzerland. He was told that the helicopter carrying Zuma was missing. A party of four were rescued after an avalanche. He switched on the tracker monitor he carried. To his great surprise there was a signal, and it was on the coast of Scotland. He felt some relief. He called Fregoli with the news.

"They'll be located and caged!" said Fregoli. He dispatched a team of mercenaries to the location.

Aboud went on deck to think. He could still come out of this on top. He continued to rub his father's ring. He would have his revenge, eliminate the threat to Xocochoc and take the Stone. It was his father's discovery, after all. Then he'd get away from these mad people. It was still and silent. A black sky dotted with countless stars was mirrored in the black loch. Like being suspended in space. "This place is well named," he said out loud to himself.

A light shone behind. He approached the porthole and looked in. He recognised the heir to the throne. Jorji appeared. She kissed the man's forehead, caressed his face, then removed the top of his head. Aboud's stomach turned inside out. He ran to his cabin and locked the door. He was fearful of losing his brain.

34

Day Seven: Poolewe by Loch Ewe

Mrs MacKenzie was passing the front door with a fresh pot of tea when four large men dressed in camouflage burst in. She was floored, scalded, hauled up and thrown into a fireside chair before she could utter a word. She had an attack of angina and pulled out her spray. Mackenzie was on his feet, a hill stick raised. He was pushed back in a chair and held by the throat. Camouflage One compared his face to the photo and nodded. Camouflage Two, the Inquisitor, smiled and said, "I hope you're not too easy, old man. I like to keep my skills well practised. Where is the piece of Stone?"

"What are you talking about?" said Mackenzie with mounting anger.

"Your wife will be strangled if you don't show us where it is," said Camouflage Two.

"Harm my mother and it'll be more than me you'll be up against."

"Good. I like threats." Camouflage Two approached MacKenzie and with a gloved hand punched him in the gut. MacKenzie doubled up.

"Stop it, you beast!" shouted Mrs Mackenzie. "Take them to the cave, Willie!"

Mrs MacKenzie knew what she was doing. She knew he couldn't remember where he'd hidden the Stone. Going to the cave on Gruinard might give him a chance to do something. And they both knew that Ian Cross, the policeman, would come to their house for tea in a short while.

He was tending to MacKenzie's sheep on the hill with Sasha, their Border collie. Camouflage Four was ordered to stay with Mrs MacKenzie. The others left with MacKenzie.

"Where is it?" asked Camouflage One when they'd pushed him into the back seat of a black Range Rover.

"Gruinard Island."

Looking at the map, Camouflage Three said, "There's a place we can land."

"You'll have to go by boat. It's in a cave that's only just accessible at low tide. That gives you less than one hour in and out," said Mackenzie.

"And you have a boat, old man?" asked Camouflage Two.

MacKenzie nodded.

Camouflage One drove to Gruinard Bay averaging eighty miles an hour, on a tortuous, high level road, scaring the pants off a dozen other motorists.

In the open boat MacKenzie sat in the stern, manning the chugging outboard. He wished for any one of three miracles: one, that he had actually hidden the Stone in the cave; two, that another tornado would come along and he'd be the lucky one again; or three, something that sent a shiver down his spine…

"That's the entrance," he said, pointing to a two-metre black opening above the water line.

"You lead, old man," said Camouflage Two, switching on a torch as they climbed out of the boat onto a slab of slimy rock sloping up to the seaweed-covered floor of the cave. Camouflage One, in the rear, slipped and fell back into the water. He cursed, pulling himself out.

The torchlight shone to a bend in the dripping slimy wall fifteen metres ahead. The smell of rotting eggs was overpowering. One of the black walls moved in the torchlight's beam. The huge pincer, as big as the business end of a roadworks' digging machine, clamped the torch carrier and bent his head back with a sickening crack. His body hung limp in the giant lobster's claw.

MacKenzie ran further into the cave. Camouflage Three drew a weapon and fired at the black shape. But a giant lobster's shell is bullet proof. With the other, slightly smaller pincer, Camouflage Three was whipped off his feet and held under water. Camouflage One repeated his flying act in a state of sheer terror and as he struggled to stand up again the huge armoured body sat on him. MacKenzie saw his chance. His brain was a bit rusty but he still had a good pair of hill legs. He was out of the cave and away in the boat in less than a minute.

"Thank God for number three!" he shouted.

35

Day Seven: Inverewe Garden by Loch Ewe

Sgian's heart sank as they approached the botanic garden. It was buried under fallen trees. The visitor centre was flattened under a mighty eucalyptus tree. A saw buzzed behind a tangle of branches. Sgian shouted to the tangle. "Where is the Inverewe birch?" The buzz stopped.

"It's by the greenhouse that's been blown away. Someone else was asking me about it. You'll never get near it," said the voice. The buzz restarted.

"What now, Sgian?" asked Hela as they walked away.

"MacKenzie showed me a tunnel that was made during the war. It goes along the top of the garden. We might get lucky and reach the tree."

The entrance to the tunnel was hidden behind a large vertical tree root. Sgian led, torch in hand. Rotten wooden slats lined the walls and floor. Roots draped in cobwebs sprouted through spaces. It was dry. They had to crouch. Fifty metres along they came to the exit in a tangle of branches.

"The gardener said it was near the greenhouse. Can you see any sign of it, Hela?" said Sgian with a smile.

She bent down and picked up a piece of broken glass. "I think this is the best I can do," she said. They peered through the branches. "I see green, Sgian."

It was the only tree standing. But the ground to one side had been excavated. Sgian's heart sank once again. No sign of the piece of Stone. Has it been taken? Maybe it's somewhere else. Then he remembered what the gardener said about someone else enquiring and MacKenzie's words to Morag MacDonald, the retired Gaelic teacher. She was one of the students who took the Stone of Destiny from Westminster Abbey. He'd said 'enchanted roots'. "I think I know who has the piece of Stone. It's on our way to the ruin," he said.

They set off for the Beaver.

36

Day Seven: Gruinard Bay

The Beaver was circling overhead, preparing to land.

"Are they still working on the ruin, Sgian?" asked Hela.

Sgian was scanning with the binoculars. "Strange, no sign of them. Wait a minute. There's something. No, there's a body on rocks." He continued the sweep. "Someone in a boat going towards the ruin."

"Here we go, Sgian. Something's wrong," said Hela.

They landed as near to the ruin as possible, raced to shore in the inflatable and ran up the beach.

"It's Lars," shouted Sgian, who got there first.

Hela checked Lars's pulse and breathing then turned him gently onto his side. One eye was swollen. His nose and upper lip were cut. There was a gash on his temple and she saw that his knuckles were badly bruised. "He's still breathing. This was no accident. I think Lars put up one hell of a fight. Let's get him to the plane. I've got medical stuff there." At that moment, the chugging outboard reached the shore and MacKenzie stepped out of the boat.

"Goodness me, what's happened?" he said as they came down the beach carrying Lars. "Put him in my boat. It'll be quicker."

Back in the Beaver, Hela the healer got to work. MacKenzie told his tale. Hela gave him her mobile and he called Ian Cross, who called his bigger brother and two fishermen home from the sea. They would deal with Camouflage Four and make sure Mrs MacKenzie came to no harm. He also told the policeman about the Professor and Fiona's disappearance.

"Shall I go and see if Morag knows about the missing piece of Stone? She lives nearby," Sgian said to Hela and MacKenzie. They both agreed.

MacKenzie looked frustrated. "I'm sorry. It's a complete blank for me. If anyone knows it will be Morag," he said. Sgian hoped so too.

Sgian ran all the way to Miss MacDonald's house. When she opened the door he knew right away she'd taken the piece of Stone.

"I was expecting you, Sgian. The Maree family were the original guardians of the Stone and I was sure you would be part of the next chapter, whatever that is. Willie could never remember where he'd hidden it, but things he said seemed to point to the Inverewe birch. So when the storm passed I took the opportunity to look. And just as well. Though the tree was still standing, the Stone had been exposed. Here it is." She uncovered the piece as it lay on a footstool.

Sgian gave her a brief description of the Swiss events and the Professor's theory. He also told her about MacKenzie's adventure and the disappearance of the Professor and Fiona.

"The Spirit of Scotland's on your side, Sgian. You'll find them and win through," she said at the door before he left.

37

Day Seven: *Britannia*

When his mercenaries failed to return from the MacKenzie operation, Fregoli had Professor Sterne brought to his State Room.

"It was unfortunate that the boy, Sgian Dubh, was not with your party when my men arrived. You and the girl might have been spared. Your Norwegian friend put up strong resistance. I am sorry for his demise. I require both pieces of the Stone of Destiny for a coronation. And like you, I'm interested in its special properties. So you will contact the boy, wherever he is, and have him brought here within the hour. The fate of your young companion hangs in the balance. Let me show you something." Fregoli took the Professor to a window and pointed to the Faraday cage containing Fiona. "Like a bird in a cage," he said, smiling.

The Professor phoned Hela and described the situation. She gave Hela the *Britannia*'s location. Hela told her that Lars was still alive and that Sgian was looking for the other piece of Stone.

"Sgian's trying to find the missing piece of Stone. No one knows where it is. I've asked that he be brought here but he may come empty handed. Then what?" said the Professor.

"I hope for all your sakes he finds it. Now I think it only fair that you keep your young friend company," said Fregoli. She was taken away. Fregoli called Aboud. "I expect the boy to arrive by plane with the missing piece of Stone in an hour. Jorji is examining the material we acquired at the ruin. You could assist her when she goes to the plane. The Professor has joined the Bellamy girl in the cage. We'll discuss their fate later."

Aboud saw a light at the end of his nightmare tunnel.

38

Day Seven: Gruinard Bay

Sgian returned to the shore with the piece of Stone in Fiona's backpack. He was ferried to the Beaver by MacKenzie. Hela broke the news.

"OK. That's the way it has to be. We go. And there's time to make a plan," said Sgian. He showed them the piece of Stone. MacKenzie was happy to hear it had been found under the Inverewe birch and that Morag had saved it. Sgian also showed Hela the bug that had been planted in Fiona's bag in Zurich before he threw it into the sea.

Hela's mobile rang. "It's Ian Cross from the police station here. Can you let Willie know that Mrs MacKenzie's fine. We've arrested the character who was holding her. He's not speaking. Willie can tell us about the others when he gets back."

"We'll fly him back to Loch Ewe shortly. There's something else. Professor Sterne and Sgian's stepsister have been kidnapped. They're being held on the *Britannia*," said Hela.

There was a pause before the policeman spoke. "*Britannia*. You mean the Royal Yacht?" he shouted. There was another pause. "I'll have to get in touch with my superiors. This is tricky. You know there's been a bit of an upheaval in Edinburgh and the Prince of Wales has been kidnapped. I have to tread carefully in these changing times."

Hela wasn't quite sure what that meant.

They flew MacKenzie back to Loch Ewe, then, before taking off for Loch Hourn, they discussed tactics.

"These people mean business. They want the Stone. But I'm sure they don't know its importance. Perhaps we can persuade them to let Anna decide how to use it?" said Hela.

"I have a feeling they're not that kind of people. Something else is going on. Even if we give them the Stone we won't be spared. Let's try to free Fiona and the Professor," said Sgian. Hela looked sceptical but had no ideas. "Knots, locks and rocks. I'm at my best when there's a struggle, Hela. Rescuing Fi and the Prof might be tricky. But we've no other option."

Hela was amazed at his calm confidence. He reminded her of a character in one of her father's Viking legends. She smiled and said, "I think you have some Viking blood, Sgian. We have an hour. Beaver can get us there in twenty-five minutes."

The Beaver took off. During the flight Sgian rummaged around the equipment at the back of the plane. As he was looking for rope an image came to mind and he put something else in the backpack.

The Beaver flew in low behind a headland. Hela switched the power off, gliding onto the dark surface of the loch.

"Take care, Sgian. I'll move close to the *Britannia* in half an hour. I'll be keeping an eye out for you," she said, holding up the binoculars.

"As the man said, I'll be back, and so will they," he replied, giving Hela a hug.

He pulled on the backpack and climbed into the inflatable.

39

Day Seven: *Britannia*

Aboud decided to get out now. He had to deal with the threat to Xocochoc. He would avenge his father's death and get both pieces of this Stone. His father had once referred to it as a power source. What did that mean? Obviously, the Professor and Fregoli knew something. He and his man would go by launch and wait on the water until the boy arrived. Then he'd deal with Jorji.

Hela taxied the Beaver to open water after thirty minutes. There was no sign of Sgian. She was on the wing doing a check. She heard the launch approaching at the last moment and made a move towards the cockpit. The silenced shot slammed into her shoulder and propelled her into the water.

"You fool. We need a live pilot. Now we'll have to get out of here by boat. And where's that boy?" Aboud shouted to his man.

They found the half Stone, went back aboard the motor launch and set off to collect the other piece from the firing chamber. Then he'd put an end to the caged 'birds'. They jumped ashore and walked up the beach. Aboud found Jorji inside the firing chamber. Obviously, she'd not heard the plane land. She was carrying out some sort of test on the piece of Stone. He'd have to get her out of the way before taking it. The answer came to him. He patted one pocket. She turned and was surprised to see Aboud and his man. She saw the plane on the loch.

"I wondered where you'd got to. And when did the plane arrive? I didn't hear it land. We should go and get the boy and the other piece of Stone," she said.

"Care to show me how the gun works first?" said Aboud.

"Nothing to it."

Jorgi described aiming and firing in detail. "…the shell is primed with nanoparticles just before firing. It's set to explode in the cloud."

"Very interesting. Like to try the world's finest chocolate?" Aboud asked.

She took a piece, then another, then another. All the while Aboud was whispering, "The boy's thrown the Stone into the loch and escaped. Montez has gone after him. You will tell that to Fregoli." He made her repeat the statement. She used her cell phone and then started to walk back to the ship.

Several minutes later, Jorji found herself wandering along the shoreline. She felt really relaxed and smiled to herself. She couldn't remember what she was doing there.

There was a loud bang. She looked round. The Faraday cage had been blown from its mooring. It was hurtling towards a rockface. She looked at the firing chamber.

Aboud and his man were loading the Stone and gold into the launch. They jumped aboard and cast off.

40

Sgian pulled on his driving gloves and climbed up *Britannia*'s bow rope. He set about exploring the ship. He was surprised not to see or hear any signs of the crew. He found a plan of the ship inside a doorway. His skill at route finding imprinted the key features in his mind. He identified several places where Fiona and the Professor might be held. Something drew him to the ship's sickbay on the main deck. He looked through a porthole.

Two figures draped in green towels were seated on operating chairs. Their faces, eyes closed, were visible. The heir to the throne had an identical twin! The dissecting neuropathfinder, a robotic surgical device, hovered on its electronic arm above them. A tall red machine stood by the doorway. One of the patients opened his eyes and looked straight into Sgian's. He recognised the chilling look of the man on Culloden field. The man must have communicated with the machine. Its top turned.

Sgian saw an eye look to the porthole. The machine moved like lightning. Sgian reacted. He ran along a passageway, through a hatch and down steps. He was on a metal walkway overlooking the engine room. He heard muffled shouting from behind a door. He knew that voice. The locked door didn't present a problem. A figure, its head in a canvas bag tied round the neck, was lashed to a chair with masking tape.

"I'll get you out of that," said Sgian, trying to put a name to the voice.

"It's you, isn't it, Sgian?" said the figure.

Sgian took the hood off. "Hamish? What? How did you get here?" he said.

"No time for that. Get the dirk oot o' my stocking and cut me loose. The Prince is a prisoner. We've got tae find him."

Sgian pulled a gold-handled sgian dubh from Hamish's stocking, cut the tape and handed the dirk back. There was a clacking sound behind. Sgian felt himself clamped round the chest, lifted up and thrown against the bulkhead. Hamish was on his feet and lunged at the robot. The two-metre tall machine clamped on the boy but the momentum of Hamish's attack carried the two figures out of the door and over the walkway above the engine room. Sgian heard the metallic crash and ran to look down. The red robot was lying motionless. Its four arms were encircling nothing.

"Hamish! Hamish, are you alright?" Sgian shouted. No reply. Out of the corner of his eye Sgian saw a red blur moving fast along the walkway towards him. He ran. He found a ladder going up two decks and bounded through a hatchway onto the upper deck. He ran aft to the stern rope and slid down, hanging by hands and feet, thanking whomever for his driving gloves. Then he sprinted. Marinebot Two took the gangway steps three at a time. Glancing round, Sgian saw the figure motoring towards him. A knife flew past the boy's head. Thud! He felt as if he'd been kicked in the back as another knife buried itself into his backpack. Sgian headed for the rough mountain terrain.

Once there, he could outrun everything other than red deer, 'Or a robot?' he thought. It was high-speed scrambling. Marinebot Two was not falling behind. He heard a loud bang. He glanced behind him. He saw a cage flying up the mountainside a few metres off the ground. It crashed onto rocks and bounced down towards a tree-covered ledge.

"If David could do it, I'll give it a go," said Sgian, snatching up a perfectly round quartz rock as his hand fell on it. Marinebot Two was ten metres behind down the slope. Its eye took the full force of the missile. The robot kept up its speed but was now running at right angles to the boy. It ran out of mountainside after twenty metres and disappeared over the edge of a cliff. Sgian looked back to where the cage had landed.

From being a perfect egg shape, the cage became a pumpkin with its top buckled open. He saw two figures inside. He used his monocular. His heart skipped a beat. Fiona and the Professor were strapped to seats.

He was whipped off his feet once again. Marinebot Three had him in its grip and motored back to the ship. It took the boy to the operating theatre where Fregoli stood in black theatre attire holding a scalpel in his purple latex-gloved hand.

"You must be Sgian Dubh. The boy who threw away the Stone and who's seen too much," said Fregoli. Sgian was still restrained by the robot. Fregoli took hold of Sgian's neck with one hand and squeezed. "Go and fetch Professor Douglas while I finish this task," he said to the machine.

Sgian struggled. He couldn't breathe. He felt as if his head were about to burst. He saw a tall figure in theatre greens walk up behind Fregoli.

Compressing the carotid sinus in the neck leads to sudden loss of consciousness. It requires an exact knowledge of the victim's anatomy. Oliver Jeffrey had that knowledge. Fregoli fell down. Sgian coughed and wheezed but recovered quickly. He didn't know who the masked person was until he spoke.

"You are kin, Sgian Dubh. I've wronged your family in the past. Go from this place. I must deal with this monster for once and for all," said Oliver Jeffrey.

Sgian ran out of the theatre. He had to jump over a headless robot in the passageway. Sgian climbed like a mountain goat. His hands and feet had minds of their own.

The Professor and Fiona were saved by the seatbelts. The cage's heavy base and egg shape kept it upright. It had crashed base first, then bounced down the side of the mountain. A clump of old rowan trees with firmly established roots had arrested its fall. It hung about a thousand metres up on a downward-slanting ledge overhanging the loch.

He reached the cage, picked the door lock and helped the Professor and Fiona onto a ledge barely a metre in width. It lay beneath an overhang. There was no way back.

"Don't look down. Hang on to the rowan," said Sgian, helping them out. Fiona had tears in her eyes. She gave him a one-arm hug and grabbed a rowan branch with the other. The Professor had a faint smile and tearful eyes. Fiona had moved a couple of steps along the ledge. Their position was precarious.

"If Sgian got up here, Fiona, I know he'll get us down," said the Professor.

Sgain took off the backpack. He pulled out two emergency parachutes and rope. Two mouths opened, but no words came.

"This is what I was going to tell you, Fiona. Since I ditched the skateboard I read a book on paragliding," he said. Eyes widened. Mouths remained open, heads slightly shaking. "Grab the roof of the cage when

I take it off."

Sgian climbed onto the roof of the cage and unscrewed the cupola that formed it. He climbed back down, stepped inside the cage, pushed the cupola off, then slid it back towards the ledge. The Professor and Fiona used their free hands to hold it. He fitted the parachutes to each of them. He kicked the cage and it tumbled over the edge.

"Sit on either side of the roof and hold on to this rope," he said. He tied a length of rope to each side of the cupola, round their waists, through the hole in the centre of the cupola and round his waist. He moved the cupola forwards to rest partly on the ledge but mainly on the rowans. Every movement by the passengers rocked the cupola. Their position was even more precarious.

The matter of fact, relaxed way Sgian went about preparing the 'craft' amazed the other two. The near-fatal encounter they'd just experienced put them into a mindset that didn't question what was about to happen. Neither of them even thought to ask whether Sgian had ever paraglided before or whether such a craft had ever been launched into space. He hadn't. It hadn't. They trusted him.

"Hang on to the rope attached to the cupola. When I shout 'pull', pull the parachute release toggles for all you're worth, then hang on to both ropes. Shout 'Geronimo' as loud as you can the moment we're airborne," said Sgian.

He pushed the cupola off the ledge. The rowan was its only support. He started turning it. Just as it tipped forwards he climbed on and with one foot pushed against the rock. He tightened the ropes round his waist.

"Geronimo!" they all shouted in unison. They flew into space and hurtled down, spinning round and wobbling. White knuckles hung on. Dry mouths yelled.

"Pull!" he shouted. The two chutes opened. Sgian grabbed the lines of both chutes.

The cupola jerked, slowed and drifted out across the water. There was a ripping sound from one shoot and the cupola started to pitch, roll and yaw like crazy. Sgian realised that the robot's dagger had pierced one chute. The cupola was on the verge of capsizing and they were still over three hundred metres up. The torn chute was only half open now.

"They call this next trick 'Big Ears'. You're meant to collapse the outer edges of both wings. I'm going to try and collapse the good chute a little bit," he shouted, trying to convince himself that he knew what he was doing. It happened. They went into a classic 'Big Ears' rapid descent.

A bolt of lightning flashed close by.

41

Day Seven: Loch Hourn

"A perfect escape from hell. Now earn your keep and get us to an airport," said Montez Aboud to his man as he sat in the motor launch cabin. Both pieces of the Stone of Destiny, with the gold piece sandwiched between them, sat on the floor beside him. The moment the two pieces had been set down beside each other they had clamped together and could not be separated. He patted the grey stone.

"I've avenged my father's death and have the prize, whatever secret it holds. But the girl's interference presents Xocochoc with a problem," he said. He used his mobile. "Flood the market with special Choxoco immediately and relocate to our standby facility," he said to someone in Zurich. "That should shake the Swiss foundations."

There was a boom. He looked out of the cabin. A cloud above the excavated mountain glowed for a moment. A bolt of lightning cracked down to the firing chamber followed by a clap of thunder. There was another bright flash as the lightning was reflected off the diamond mirror.

The intense flash that followed blinded Aboud and his man a millisecond before flesh and boat evaporated. The Stone of Destiny and gold sgian glowed white-hot as they sank to the bottom of the loch.

Hela had a superficial wound to one shoulder and was back aboard the Beaver. She saw a weird-looking paraglider doing dangerous manoeuvres. She saw a motor launch speeding across the loch. She saw a woman running along the shore.

Jorji covered two hundred metres of beach in thirty seconds. She ran into the firing chamber and sat at the control panel. A jet of supercooled water vapour was blasted to the mountain's summit and formed a cloud. She loaded a nanoshell, aimed the gun at the cloud and fired. She adjusted the large diamond mirror. The lightning bolt shot down, bounced off the mirror and flashed horizontally across the loch towards the motor launch.

Hela saw a flash, heard a clap of thunder, another flash and saw the motor launch disappear in a ball of flame. She grabbed her binoculars and watched the paraglider approach the water. She saw it had Team Beaver on board. She jumped into her seat, fired up the engine and taxied towards them.

42

Day Seven: The *Britannia* Operating Theatre

Oliver Jeffrey stooped over Fregoli and compressed both carotid arteries to finish his task. A primitive survival reflex moved Fregoli's arm, still clutching the scalpel. It penetrated Oliver Jeffrey's eye socket and entered the brain. Both men died. One on top of the other.

Jorji burst in to the theatre. Some instinct told her what had happened. She pulled the green-gowned figure off Fregoli, felt for his carotid pulse then screamed. She looked at the other man's face, realised it wasn't Professor Douglas and rushed out of the theatre. She found him bound and gagged in his cabin. He was released and brought to the theatre.

"You will proceed with the personality transplant as planned. But first you will transplant Fregoli's intellect into The Pretender. I will assist. If you fail in any way I shall kill you," she said.

The slightly built Professor knew he was no match for this female.

43

On board the plane they recovered, drank coffee and talked about events for some time.

Suddenly Sgian had a forewarning. "Take off now! The Stone's been struck," he shouted.

They all looked at him and understood. Hela switched on the power. The Beaver lifted off.

It started quietly. A gentle swell on a windless day. Bubbles appeared here and there. Shafts of light flashed from the deep. The black loch sparkled. Jets of water burst into the air, tumbling down as phosphorescent cascades. Deep rumbling sounds. Explosions on the surface as if from depth charges. Huge waves rolled towards the shores from every direction. Tidal chaos. Countless whirlpools. The loch was boiling. A pulsing green glow came from its depths. The land around the loch began to shake. Steaming mud, plants, fish and glowing, hissing rocks were thrown up from the depths as faults in the Earth's crust were wrenched apart. The gates of hell opened.

Chemical weathering of calcium silicate in rocks absorbs CO_2 from the atmosphere and takes place over millennia. The lightning strike on the gold sgian triggered a fast weathering chain reaction of CO_2 absorption by rocks. It progressed along fault lines. Rocks exploded. Slabs tumbled. Crevices opened. Stone shoots descended. Atmospheric changes followed.

The Promethean Power Company's project disintegrated.

Scotland is traversed by more than forty geological fault lines. Like cracks running through a pane of glass, the chain reaction opened the Earth's crust. The effect was greatest in a fault by Loch Hourn. Tremors were felt from the Hebrides to the Solway.

44

Britannia's starboard side was hit by waves of increasing size. Four camouflaged men jumped into the water on the port side. Team Beaver saw three people running to the stern rail as a giant wave struck. The ship went over. Waves went over the ship.

As if a switch was turned off, the loch became quiet and the waves disappeared. One body wearing a green coat came to the surface. The Beaver landed. The Professor and Sgian jumped into an inflatable and powered towards it. They pulled a man on board and wrapped him in a space blanket. He seemed to be quite unaffected by the near drowning.

On board the Beaver they recognised who he was. Middle aged, greying hair, ruddy complexion and hesitant speech. He thanked them. His gaze lingered on Sgian for a millisecond longer than on the others.

"My name's Charles. I'm most grateful. You've done us a great service. I can call on the services of the RAF for your injured friend there," he said, pointing to Lars who was coming round.

Sergeant Cross, his brother and three fishermen exploded out of a police Range Rover, rushed to the quayside, pulled the spluttering camouflaged figures from the water and cuffed them. Two of them bore the after effects of Lars's fists.

Within ten minutes of the Prince's call, two fighter jets flew over. Twenty minutes later two helicopters were hovering nearby. Lars and the heir to the throne were winched up and the helicopters flew off.

A coastguard launch and Royal Naval fishery protection vessel came up the loch at high speed and put men on board the Royal Yacht. She lay on her side with her superstructure against ruined harbour installations. Clearance divers didn't find any bodies.

The coastguards took Ian Cross to the Beaver. "Sorry we took so long to get here, folks. My superiors told me not to get involved. So we came. Then these quakes started happening everywhere. We had quite a few diversions. Looks like you were just in time for the VIP. And MacKenzie told me to say he hoped the magic worked, whatever that means." Team Beaver smiled.

He left. They flew. One hour into the Beaver's flight they received a message to say that Lars was being treated in Edinburgh's neurosurgical unit.

Another item of news was relayed. The Palace of Holyrood had been stormed by Special Forces and the attempted Jacobite coup was ended.

45

One Week Later: Edinburgh

Earth scientists reported a decrease in atmospheric CO_2 levels and temperatures in the Northern Hemisphere. There was great interest in discovering the mechanism. It presented a possible solution to climate change. The CO_2-dependent black lichen was dying. The mutant creatures were disappearing. Trees were recovering.

Sgian and Fiona took the lift up to the neurosurgical unit. They were visiting Lars.

"Shouldn't we invite Vicky for lunch, Fi?" asked Sgian.

"My thought too. I've tried her mobile several times. Left a message."

The Norwegian was recovering but still had some amnesia. They were telling him about Loch Hourn when Jude Wylie, neurosurgeon, joined them. Sgian introduced Fi.

"Hi. Great to see you both. Lars told me about Switzerland. What else happened?" Jude said.

"Remember the Gaelic words you heard Willie say?" Jude nodded. "They were a key part of the story. We saw Willie. He's fine and sends his regards," said Sgian.

"Come and have lunch with us. Then you'll get the full story," said Fiona.

"Sounds good," Jude replied.

"What happened to Willie? He can't remember meeting the Prince," said Sgian.

"It's a tangled web. I don't understand, Sgian. Strange thing. We removed something weird from his head after the tornado. Someone stole it then disappeared. My boss, Prof Douglas, was kidnapped and he's still missing. The ambulance, its crew, Willie and the nurses didn't return after the Botanic visit. We found Willie in the gents' loo, hypothermic and unconscious. No trace of the others or the ambulance. Police are still on the case. What with the tornado and the scary black lichen epidemic, the attack on ITU and the attempted Jacobite coup, I think the Scots have had enough excitement for a while. And so have I. So where are we going for lunch?" asked Jude as they walked into the surgeon's office.

"The Swiss Consul's invited us all to *Centotre*," said Fiona.

"Italian. My favourite food!" said Jude.

The restaurant was heaving. Music, chatter, laughter and the mouth-watering aromas of Italian cooking. Jude, Sgian, Fiona, her brother Mike, Mairi, Fritz and their host, Mr Mercet, enjoyed lunch. Mr Mercet raised his glass. "The lunch was a thank-you for Fritz's recovery and Fiona and Sgian's help in stopping the spread of a dangerous product. Xocochoc was raided but they'd cleared out. Sadly, my friend, Emile Fankhauser, who was involved in the operation, fell from his motor boat and was drowned."

Sgian and Fiona exchanged glances.

"What about the bugs and nanostuff?" asked Fiona.

"That's interesting, Fiona. We know that those who crave chocolate have special bacteria in their intestines. The sample you took from the factory told us everything. Choxoco had smart nanoparticles and bacteria that could turn everyone into a chocoholic. High doses could produce other psychological effects. The nanoceuticals were in the gold foil and activated by handling. We made one worrying discovery. Seeds from a giant cocoa pod had been propagated and have been used in chocolate production. They were contaminated by a black lichen. An attic space in the factory was covered in it. If that stuff is spread it could destroy the chocolate industry."

A police officer appeared at the door, looked at Sgian and approached their table. Sgian was ready to bolt.

"Sorry for interrupting. My name's MacHugh. I came to give a belated thanks to Sgian. His actions at the roadworks a couple of weeks ago were highly commendable. And I've been instructed to tell you and your sister that you'll shortly receive a communication from Holyrood Palace. Something to do with rescuing a VIP," he said.

Fiona smiled. Sgian gave a sigh of relief. The others clapped.

The policeman shook hands with Fiona and Sgian. "Well done, both of you. Enjoy your lunch," he said, then left.

Sgian was on his way to the loo and saw the reflection of a woman in the wall mirror. She was suntanned with black hair and bright red lipstick. She sat at the bar drinking coffee. Her eyes were firmly fixed on his back.

When he returned she was gone. A newspaper was lying open beside the empty lipsticked cup. One article was outlined: 'Norwegian research submarine missing in Arctic.' Sgian's heart sank.

When the family returned home they found a letter addressed to Sgian that had been posted four days earlier. He read the name and address on the back of the envelope. His hands were shaking. 'Anna Sterne, Hyerdahl Str., Oslo'. He opened it and read out loud: "Dear Sgian, You may have read reports about the loss of the submarine in the Arctic Ocean. It is *Rodt Foks* with my team on board. I still remember your words last year warning me not to go near icebergs. Had it not been for you and Fiona asking for our help in Switzerland, Lars and I would have been on board. My grief is so great at the moment …" Sgian's tears stopped him reading further. He felt both sadness and relief. Fiona took him by the shoulders. After a few minutes she read the rest of the letter: "Tell Fiona the asteroid's been named after her father. The full story will be presented at a meeting in Zurich to which you're both invited. I'll be in touch. Love Anna xx."

That evening, as he lay on his bed, Sgian's eyes went in and out of focus as he tried to read the paragliding book. His head felt fuzzy. His eyes closed. The book fell out of his hands. Purdie jumped on to the foot of the bed, curled up and closed her eyes.

Down the hallway, Fiona flopped onto her bed. Her mind was spinning from recent events. She fell asleep. She didn't feel the draught of cool air as her bedroom window opened. A moment later she was struggling in a nightmare. But it was a real cushion that was suffocating her.

Sgian jolted wide awake. So did Purdie. He rushed out of the door, ran down the hall and burst into Fiona's room. A hooded figure was suffocating Fiona. He leapt on the assailant. They both fell to one side. The hooded head caught the corner of Fiona's PC desk and lay still.

Fiona was gasping and crying. Sgian got up and took her in his arms.

They stayed like that for a few moments before Sgian bent over the figure and pulled down the hood. Vicky had a crew cut. She came round. Sgian and Fiona sat her in a chair.

"Hi, Fi, Sgi! Where is this? What's happened?" Then she caught sight of herself in Fiona's full-length mirror. "My God!" She ran one hand through her hair. "Who's done this? Oh my head hurts."

Vicky thought she was still in Switzerland. She had complete amnesia for everything since the meal in Restaurant Zeughauskeller.

46

Sgian awoke with a headache. He would rather have stayed in bed. Mairi had taken a call from the Head's office just after Fiona and Mike left, so he was getting ready for school and another session with the Head.

"Where's my bag, Mum?" he shouted downstairs.

"I threw it in the bin yesterday. It was ripped and filthy. I've got a new one for you down here," she replied.

"You what! Fiona gave it to me." he shouted, running downstairs. He ran out the back, threw open the bin and retrieved the bag. "This bag's got a lot more life left in it."

Sgian didn't like new things. He opened it to put his paragliding book and school books in. Then he saw something inside and was stunned! He had seen Hamish.

The gold-handled sgian dubh lay at the bottom. He stared at it for a couple of minutes before sliding it down the side of his sock. He threw the books and a pair of gloves in his bag and left the house, shouting over his shoulder, "See you later, Mum."

Lachlan MacCafferty was getting out of his father's new car by the school gate.

"I got these for you, Lachlan. They'll remind your dad that you need a car of your own. They're useful for other things," said Sgian, handing him a pair of driving gloves bearing the Swiss flag.

Lachlan pulled them on and smiled. "Sgi, you're a real mate. I'm glad old Robbie's admitted his mistake," he said.

"I'm off to his office now. See you, Lachlan."

The Head looked embarrassed. His face was flushed. "Emm…yes. Sgian, it seems that emm… there must have been a bit of misunderstanding the last time we met. You did very well for the school by your actions at that roadworks' business. Emm…I hope your Swiss trip was enjoyable. You deserved it," he said and stood up.

Sgian hadn't heard a word. His eyes were fixed on the crossed swords of Culloden on the Head's map.

"Oh, I almost forgot. Someone, who wished to remain anonymous, has organised a place for you on a paragliding course next weekend. Here's the paperwork. You can get back to your class now," said the Head.

Sgian stood up, took the envelope, nodded and left.

47

They would all remember this day.

Purdie came into the kitchen alone. Mairi called upstairs. No reply. Fiona and Mike had already left for school. She went upstairs. He was still asleep. But she couldn't rouse him. The doctor was called. Sgian was admitted to the Royal Infirmary. Mairi got in touch with Fiona. They decided to find out what was going on before telling Mike.

When Judith Wylie, the neurosurgeon on call, saw him in the assessment unit, her heart sank. An MRI confirmed her worst fears. She sat in a room with Mairi and Fiona.

"I think Sgian has a brain tumour," she said. There was complete silence for a few seconds. Then tears. Mairi couldn't speak.

"Can you save him, Jude?" Fiona managed to say.

"I just don't know. It depends on so many things."

"How long has it been…?" Mairi couldn't finish.

"It might have been there for some time," Jude replied.

"Would he not have known or felt something? He never said…" said Fiona.

"You know how he was. Shrugged things off. Sometimes there are no symptoms till late on."

"Sgi never gives up. Do your best, Jude," said Fiona. She turned and hugged Mairi. Jude joined them.

Sgian was facing the struggle of his life.

48

Sgian lay unconscious in a neuro intensive-care room. Drips in both arms and attached to a ventilator, his muscles were paralysed by drugs.

Angry shouting. Terrified screams. Fist punches. Falling down, down into darkness. Plunging into icy water. Ghastly, glowing, gnashing teeth. Faces flashed by. Images and sounds bombarded him. Sgian's mental underworld was busy. He rushed through his past life at high speed, experiencing all the fear, pain and uncertainty. None of the good stuff. Then, suddenly, nothingness, as if his life were on hold. Faint shimmering lights started to come towards him. He heard a distant soothing voice. The words were strange. He felt as if he were floating, completely relaxed. Messages from the brain 'tumour' were rearranging Sgian's subconscious. Memories were being intensified. Senses were heightened. Reflexes finely tuned. Unused connecting neurones in his brain's white matter burst into life. And the 'tumour' was melting away.

Sgian heard the beep beep of a monitor. He heard footsteps coming along a corridor. A door opened. He'd never heard sounds so clearly. Someone came close to him. There was a faint perfume aroma. He sensed danger but could not open his eyes. He heard a glass vial being broken and the suction of a syringe drawing up a liquid. He heard someone running.

Fiona ran. She was sure she'd heard Sgian's voice. There was no one at the nurses' station. She saw that the door to Sgian's room was open.

Half an hour earlier, Fiona had suddenly awakened at home, called a taxi and told the driver to put his foot down. She stepped into Sgian's room and saw a nurse about to plunge a needle attached to a syringe full of clear liquid into an IV line running to Sgian's arm. Without thinking, Fiona leapt forward and wrenched the hand and syringe back. The masked nurse turned, shot a venomous look into Fiona's eyes and then was gone. Fiona pressed the emergency button above the bed. Within ten seconds two nurses appeared, followed five minutes later by the neuro doctor on call. He called the neurosurgeon. Hospital security was alerted. The intruder was not found.

The neuro doctor picked up the empty glass vial and full syringe from the floor.

"Concentrated potassium solution causes cardiac arrest. You saved his life, Fiona," said the young doctor. Fiona was silent. Intuition and instinct had kicked in. But what awakened her from sleep?

Jude Wylie appeared and was quickly updated. She examined the back of Sgian's eyes and shook her head in amazement. "This is unbelievable. The pressure inside his head's returned to normal. Reverse the muscle relaxant. Get an emergency MRI done," she said to the clinical team. "You and something I don't understand have worked a miracle, Fiona. Why was someone trying to kill him?"

Fiona shook her head. "I don't know. I can't even explain what made me rush here through the night."

The scan was done. Jude was stunned as she looked at the images. "That so-called brain tumour's less than a quarter of the size it was yesterday. It's almost as if Sgian has some sort of unique antitumour mechanism," she said.

Sgian was extubated. He opened his eyes and smiled. Fiona gave him a hug. She explained what had happened. He was nodding. "Someone was speaking to me. The words were strange. I asked you to come and help me understand. Then I heard and smelt someone come to the bedside. It's a perfume I'll recognise again. I'm lucky to have you lot looking after me," he said in a hoarse voice.

Jude's mobile rang. "Whoever it was got away, but the police are on the case. They think it's something to do with you rescuing the royal. Maybe it was one of the Jacobites. You'll probably be under police surveillance for a while after you get home," she said.

Just what Sgian didn't need!

"I hope you'll let me go soon," he said.

"We need to repeat the scan and try to make a diagnosis. But it won't be long."

"Could I ask a favour of someone? My back's itchy," said Sgian.

He sat up. A nurse went to rub his back and with a shocked expression signalled Jude to look. There was a gold tattoo over his upper spine. Jude asked Fiona to look.

"It's the mark of the gold sgian," she said.

Sgian was nodding. "You know what, Fi? My back was burning when I carried MacKenzie's piece of Stone in your backpack."

"So has that got something to do with the brain tumour, Jude?" asked Fiona.

"It's a mystery, but I'm sure it's linked to recent events," said Jude.

"Some pieces of our jigsaw are still missing then, Sgi?" said Fiona with a quizzical look.

"Or maybe one or two are not what they seem," he replied. There was something in the back of his mind he couldn't quite reach.